CHESSIE

a Short Novel

written by:

Robert G. Thayer

ISBN: 979-8-9916030-2-7 (Paperback)
ISBN: 979-8-9916030-0-3 (Hardcover)

Library of Congress Control Number: 2024920382

Front cover image and Book design by Robert G. Thayer

First printing edition 2024.

Thayer Entertainment
Robert G. Thayer
25290 Calvert Drive
Greensboro, MD 21639

www.thayerfilm.com

This, my first book, is dedicated to
my Mother-in-Law

Kathie Brooks
who truly believes in anything I do.

I thank and appreciate my many proofreaders!

Kathie Brooks
Donna Eveland
Marie U'Ren
Wendy Thayer
Pamela Bishop
Jennifer Seifert
Robin Thayer
Danuta Olson-Schuessler
Valerie Marchand Welsh

Prologue

There's a tale that drifts through the annals of Chesapeake Bay, as old as the wooded banks and just as slippery. It speaks of a creature, Chessie by name, who's said to be a sea monster not unlike the Loch Ness beast of Scotland. But where Nessie prowls the lochs, Chessie takes her leisure in the sprawling, misty waters of the Bay.

Now, Chessie's more than just a figment of folklore; she's a spirit of the waters, as elusive and as essential as love itself. Like that potent elixir flowing through our veins, she's nearly vanished, slipping away from sight like morning fog when captured or confined. Yet, in the boundless expanse of the Chesapeake's watery labyrinth, she might still be lurking, her legend still alive in the hearts of those who dare to believe.

Chapter 1

"Robert's Home"

St. Michaels, Maryland, was not just a name on a map, but a place forever etched in history as "The Town that Fooled the British." Yet, for young Robert, it was more than a town of legends; it was where the story of his life began, a tale woven with threads of loss and love.

Robert entered the world at a steep price—his mother passed on the day he was born, and his father, as folks around town said, followed her soon after, his heart too broken to carry on. At least, that was the way Grandma told it, and she was the one who took him in, raising him from the time he was barely a year old. Her house stood firm amongst the 19th-century homes of old watermen and shipbuilders on Water Street, a place where the smell of saltwater and wood mingled in the air.

This waterfront home, once a vacation haven for his parents, now belonged to Robert, with Grandma as the custodian until he came of age. A sturdy but weathered dock reached out from the yard into the West St. Michaels Harbor, offering passage to the Miles River, the Eastern Bay, the Chesapeake, and beyond. It was the kind of place that made you feel like the whole world was within reach if you just knew how to set sail.

Robert's parents, high-minded attorneys from Washington D.C., had met at Harvard, two bright stars crossing paths before fading too soon. But on this particular Sunday morning, none of that was on Robert's mind.

"Bobby?" Grandma's voice floated down the hallway, gentle but insistent, as she made her way toward his room. The sun had barely risen, and yet here she was, calling him to get ready for church. She rapped lightly on his door before opening it, finding Robert already dressed, his shirt tucked in, and his tie knotted just so, as he combed his damp hair in front of the mirror.

"Ready, Grandmother," he said, his voice steady, as he reached for a bottle of cologne on his dresser and dabbed a bit on his neck.

Grandma smiled, stepping behind him to straighten his tie with the practiced hands of a woman who had seen many Sundays come and go. "Well, don't you look handsome!" she remarked, her eyes meeting his in the mirror. "In all my days, I've never seen a young man so eager to get to church. Now hurry on, I've made you some egg sandwiches."

She left him with a smile, but Robert's thoughts were elsewhere as he followed her down to the kitchen.

Chapter 2

"Church and Such"

The St. Michaels Mission Church on Lincoln Avenue wasn't just a place where folks gathered to bow their heads and murmur their prayers; it was also where young Robert found himself spending many a Sunday, both in pew and classroom. On this particular Sunday, he sat beside his Grandma, smack dab in the middle of the chapel, his eyes as busy as a cat at a mouse hole. Grandma, sharp as a tack, noticed how his attention wandered not to the altar, but to the faces filing through the doors.

As the mass began and the last of the latecomers shuffled to their seats, Robert's eyes kept roving, scanning the rows of worshipers with a look that grew more and more forlorn as the moments passed. It was as if he was hoping to see someone in particular, but that someone had yet to make an appearance.

Grandma, sensing his distraction, gave him a firm tap on the knee. Her voice was barely above a whisper, but it had the weight of a command. "Stop fidgeting and pay attention. You're being rude."

Robert straightened up, but his thoughts were far from the sermon. He tried to focus, but his mind had already slipped out of the chapel and into a place where daydreams took root.

After the service, it was time for Sunday School, where the children were herded into separate rooms to crack open their Bibles and ponder the lessons within. This was where Robert met some of the kids from the public school—new faces from out of town who brought with them tales and rumors that always seemed more interesting than scripture.

But Robert's interest in these newcomers paled in comparison to one particular sight that greeted him when he stepped into his classroom—Lisa. There she was, the girl who had somehow caught hold of his young heart, with her dark hair and those baby blue eyes that seemed to see right through him. In a room full of other children, it was Lisa who stood out, the one face among many that made his heart skip a beat.

Lisa was a sight to behold brunette hair that shimmered in the light and baby blue eyes that seemed to pull you in without trying. The first time Robert laid eyes on her, something inside him shifted, like a compass needle finding its true north. He hadn't expected to see her in class that day; after all, he hadn't noticed her family at church. But here she was, right in front of him, as if the stars had aligned just for this moment.

Robert knew she lived somewhere in St. Michaels, though he hadn't yet mustered the courage to speak more than a few shy words in the weeks since he first saw her. But today was different. Today, he slipped into his seat directly across from her with a heart that pounded loud enough to drown out the world.

Whenever Lisa glanced away, Robert found his eyes drawn to her like a moth to a flame. She wore a white sweater that seemed to glow, paired with a long maroon skirt that added to her elegance. Everything about her was perfect—the way she smiled, the way her teeth shone like pearls, the way she seemed to float rather than walk. He was entranced, caught up in a spell he couldn't—and didn't want to—break.

But with that enchantment came a flood of worries. What would he say to her? What if she didn't like him? What if he said something foolish? His mind swirled with questions until, without warning, the moment came crashing down.

"Why are you staring at me, Bobby?" Lisa whispered, catching him in the act.

Robert felt his face flush every shade of red there was. "What? Oh, I don't know. I can't help it. I'm sorry," he stammered, feeling like the biggest fool in the world.

To his surprise, Lisa smiled, a blush creeping into her cheeks as well.

But Robert couldn't shake the feeling that his response was utterly stupid. He stewed in his own embarrassment, feeling like he'd just dug himself into a hole he might never climb out of. Ignoring the nun droning on about the day's lesson, he reached into his pocket for a note he had prepared for just such an occasion.

Chapter 3

"The Note"

"Pssst, Lisa?" he whispered, trying to catch her attention again. "I wrote this for you." He slid the note across the table, his heart pounding. But before Lisa could grab it, Sister Maria swooped in like a hawk, snatching the note right out of his hand.

"What is this, Bobby?" she asked, unfolding the paper with a look that could freeze the Chesapeake Bay.

"I'm sorry, Sister Maria. That's a note for Lisa," Robert mumbled, feeling the blood drain from his face.

"Oh? Since you feel my class time is your time to communicate with your friends, perhaps you can share the note with all of us," Sister Maria said, her voice dripping sternly.

Lisa buried her face in her arms, clearly mortified, while Robert sat frozen, wishing the floor would open up and swallow him whole.

Sister Maria wasn't about to let him off the hook. She dragged his chair to the front of the room. "C'mon, let's go. You've wasted enough of our time already. Stand up and read what was so important to the entire class."

With trembling hands, Robert took the note from her and stood before the small chalkboard, his heart beating like a drum in his ears. Sister Maria loomed over his shoulder, and she started him off with a nudge.

"Let's go, Bobby. 'Dear Lisa,'" she prompted.

Robert swallowed hard and began to read. "'Dear Lisa, I do not know why I am writing this. What I do know is that since I first saw you, I cannot think of anything else that makes me as happy.'"

The class erupted in laughter, and Robert's cheeks burned with shame. But Sister Maria wasn't having it.

"Children, not a sound from any of you. Please, Bobby, finish."

Lisa, who had been hiding her face, lifted her head slightly, her eyes fixed on Robert with something like admiration. She saw now that he meant every word.

Robert continued, "'I did not know God could make someone as beautiful as you—your beautiful eyes. I wonder what your beautiful smile looks like in the rain and the snow. I wonder about you all the time. I wonder if it would be okay to walk you to school sometimes. Maybe go canoeing or fishing together or whatever you like to do. you can come with me to the Crab Claw Restaurant this afternoon for some Mudd Pie if you like it, or whatever you like. Please let me know. It is always nice seeing you again, Bobby.'"

"Now, if you're finished disrupting my class, take your seat, Bobby," Sister Maria said, dismissing him with a wave.

Robert trudged back to his chair, his face burning, his eyes fixed on the floor. He could feel all the girls staring at him and the boys struggling not to laugh out loud. He felt like crying, humiliated beyond measure when suddenly he felt something brush against his leg under the table.

He looked down and saw it was Lisa's foot. Slowly, he raised his eyes to meet hers, and to his astonishment, she was smiling at him, tears glistening in her eyes. She nodded ever so slightly, a silent "yes" to his clumsy invitation.

Robert could hardly believe it. She had said yes! At that moment, he thought nothing in the world could ever make him feel this glorious again.

Chapter 4

"Young Love"

From that moment on, Robert and Lisa were as inseparable as two peas in a pod. They walked to school together, rode their bikes along the dusty roads of St. Michaels, canoed down the winding rivers, fished in the quiet coves, and even took up dancing lessons together, much to the amusement of their friends. They were a pair as natural as sunshine and blue skies. At just eleven years old, they even went into business together—a venture that combined the charm of their small town with their youthful ingenuity.

Now, St. Michaels, as every local will proudly tell you, is known as "The Town that Fooled the British." Back in 1812, when the Royal Navy aimed to bombard the town, the clever residents hung lanterns high in the treetops, tricking the British into over-shooting with their cannon fire. Robert and Lisa, ever the enterprising duo, decided to tap into that storied past. All winter long, they worked side by side in Robert's garage, smithing cannonballs from scraps of metal. They melted down whatever they could find and poured it into molds, crafting cannonballs that looked as aged as the town's history itself. Lisa had a knack for giving them that perfect patina of authenticity. When summer rolled around, they hit the bustling sidewalks of Talbot Street, mingling with the throngs of tourists and selling those cannonballs as relics "discovered" in the fields.

But as with all tales, there came a time when outside forces threatened the course of their relationship. Lisa, who had chosen to stay in St. Michaels as a waitress rather than pursue college, found herself at the center of Robert's deepest fears. While he was away at Harvard Law School, the absence of her beauty, smile, and kiss left a void in his life, though it allowed him to focus on his studies. However, when Robert returned home one summer, he discovered that other suitors eagerly vied for Lisa's affection. Her mother mentioned that Lisa had been working and spending time with friends, and Robert couldn't help but wonder if her heart had wandered.

The harbor in those days was a sea of twinkling mast lights, with sailboats packed so tightly together on weekend nights that it seemed you could walk across the water on their decks. Now a seasonal waitress at the Crab Claw Restaurant, Lisa often told Robert that the wealthy sailboaters tipped better when they thought the waitresses were available. She knew how to flirt just enough to make the older men feel young again, but she was careful to keep Robert away from the restaurant when she worked. She didn't want him to see her in that light or think she might be interested in anyone else. Robert, for his part, believed she only had eyes for him. But that belief was tested one evening when he found her at a table with friends outside the old Perry Cabin Hotel.

The Perry Cabin, much grander now than it once was, was where the local waitstaff, chefs, and steamers gathered to unwind after a long night of serving tourists. Robert stood at a distance, his heart sinking as he watched Lisa, more stunning at 22 than ever before, laughing with another young man who seemed far too charming for Robert's liking.

Dark jealousy stirred in his veins—a feeling he had never known before like a thief had snatched away his very soul. Swallowing his anger, he stood just close enough to be noticed, watching her with a mix of longing and dread.

Lisa didn't need to see Robert to know he was there. She could feel his presence like an electric current, and when her eyes finally found him, her face lit up with a joyful surprise. Without a second thought, she leaped up from the table, her swollen feet forgotten, and ran to him, throwing herself into his arms with a fervor that left no room for doubt. She kissed him all over, right there in front of everyone, making it clear that he was the only man who mattered.

Chapter 5

"Me or Not"

Later that night, they found themselves on the balcony of the Hooper Strait Lighthouse, lying on their backs and gazing up at the stars. It was a familiar spot they had often snuck onto for some alone time. But tonight, Robert couldn't help but ask the question that had been gnawing at him all evening. "So, who was that good-looking guy you were hanging out with tonight?"

Lisa sat up, her eyes narrowing as she looked at him. "Why, Bobby, are we jealous?"

Robert tried to keep his voice steady, but the sadness and anger were hard to hide. "Is there a reason for me to be? It looked like you two would make a great couple."

Lisa sighed, her face softening. "Now, you listen to me, Robert. When I said I was your girl, I meant it. If you doubt how true I am, you might run off and try to do better."

"I just never saw you so happy with someone else before," Robert admitted. "At least, not with another young man."

"That's because when you're around, you're the only young man I want to be with," Lisa replied, her voice firm but tender.

Robert searched her eyes, finding the sincerity he needed. "I just want you to be happy. It's either me or it's not. I'll give you my all, but I need you to do the same."

Lisa smiled, relief washing over her. "That's just peachy because that young man you're so worried about wouldn't be interested in me anyway."

"Any man in his right mind would be," Robert said, still uncertain.

"Not this one," Lisa said with a mischievous grin.

"Why not?" Robert asked, confusion spreading across his face.

"Because I'm not man enough for him," Lisa laughed, watching as the realization and relief dawned on Robert's face.

Robert felt a mix of embarrassment and gratitude. "I'm sorry, Lisa. I shouldn't have doubted you."

Lisa placed a finger over his lips. "Hush now. No more talk of that." She kissed a tear from his cheek, then kissed him on the lips, resting her head on his chest as they lay together under the stars.

Chapter 6

"New York City"

Two years later, Robert graduated from Harvard, second in his class, and that summer, he and Lisa were married. Even Sister Maria, the old nun who had once embarrassed Robert by reading his love letter aloud, attended the wedding and reread that very note as part of the ceremony.

Within nine years, Robert found himself sitting atop a mountain of money so high, he could scarcely see the bottom. He had wrangled himself a seven-figure salary at one of those big-shot corporate law firms in Manhattan, and if that wasn't enough to make a man feel like the king of the world, they went ahead and threw in another seven-figures for Christmas, as if the first pile wasn't already more than any reasonable soul could spend in a lifetime. If Robert had ever had a money problem before, he sure as sugar wasn't going to have one again, not in this life or the next.

Shortly after settling in Manhattan, their daughter Jennifer was born. As she grew, Jennifer and her young mother delighted in the shops, Broadway shows, and restaurants that only New York City could offer. Their bond grew extraordinarily strong as Robert's long hours at the firm kept him away more often than he liked.

For Lisa, the city's excitement was a far cry from the quiet life of St. Michaels. But nothing thrilled her more than the gift Robert gave her on their ninth Christmas together—a convertible Ferrari in her favorite shade of blue. She loved cruising through its city streets, feeling like she owned the world.

Since the Ferrari was about as useful in city traffic as a screen door on a submarine, Lisa reckoned it was time to let the flashy beast go. She didn't shed too many tears over it, though. Practicality called, and she answered with a top-of-the-line Mercedes Benz—a car just as luxurious, but one that wouldn't make her feel like she was trying to thread a needle with boxing gloves every time she hit downtown.

Saturday was Lisa's day. She'd head to the gym while Robert spent time with Jennifer. On one such rainy winter evening, Lisa took the Ferrari out. The streets were already dark by six o'clock when she stopped at a red light just a block from their apartment. That's when everything changed.

A loud crash shattered the night as her window broke, and before she could react, she felt the cold barrel of a gun pressed against her head.

"Get the hell out of the car, bitch!" a disheveled man snarled, his voice sharp with desperation.

Stunned and terrified, Lisa refused to leave the car, which Robert had given her, symbolizing their love and life together.

"Get out, or I'll shoot you right here, right now! I ain't playing," the man threatened.

But instead of complying, Lisa floored the car in gear. The man fired two shots as the Mercedes sped off, only to crash into a magazine stand moments later. The man fled into the night, leaving Jennifer's mother and Robert's soulmate gone forever.

Devastated, Robert left New York and returned to the family home on Water Street in St. Michaels, where he and Jennifer have lived for years. Now a widower, Robert works as a waterman, more for the novelty than the need, given his wealth. As an attorney, he's been repeatedly re-elected President of the local Watermen's Association, fighting for the rights of those who make their living on the water.

But Robert lives like an oyster, trapped within a shell of self-blame and grief, haunted by the loss of Lisa. And what's worse, he's raising a sixteen-year-old daughter alone, a girl whose looks and demeanor remind him more of her mother with each passing day.

At this point, the seemingly impossible becomes possible, where the legend of Chessie begins.

Chapter 7

"Bucky"

It was three o'clock in the morning, or thereabouts, on a moon-lit night at Perry Cove, a place so sleepy it could've passed for a bedbug's sanctuary. In all its silvery glory, the full moon threw a ghostly glow over the water, making it shimmer like a blanket of star-dusted frost. The murky depths of the cove held secrets more profound than the local gossip, and right then, something unseen was stirring beneath the surface.

Indeed, the cove had its share of eerie sounds. From the depths came low, whale-like moans, a tune that seemed too strange to be natural yet too compelling to dismiss. Once anchored firmly to the cove's muddy bottom, the wooden workboat now trembled as if caught in some mighty, unseen grasp. The anchor rope creaked and strained, and slowly, like a stubborn old man being dragged out of bed, the boat began its reluctant journey from the cove's embrace.

As if on cue, the workboat, a vessel sturdy and unyielding in daylight, was gently but insistently drawn away from the cove's quiet sanctuary. Chessie—or whatever it was—made its presence felt most unceremoniously.

Across town in sleepy Saint Michaels, where the only thing moving faster than a turtle was a stray cat, the glow of electric candles illuminated colonial windows, casting long shadows on the otherwise dim Main Street.

Sheriff Hank Royals, a man whose age seemed to have caught up with him in both spirit and physique, snored heartily behind the wheel of his patrol car. The car's engine purred softly, and a talk radio station droned on, oblivious to the slumbering sheriff.

But as fate would have it, or perhaps sheer mischief, the tranquility was shattered. A car, engines roaring and wheels squealing, came to a sudden and jarring stop in front of the sheriff's patrol car. The high beams of the vehicle cut through the night like a blinding spotlight, and Sheriff Royals, startled from his snooze, ducked beneath the dashboard, his eyes as wide as saucers.

The offending vehicle, a sorry-looking contraption that looked like it had seen better days in a junkyard, screeched to a halt just inches from the sheriff's window. The driver, a young rascal named Bucky Peterson, leaned out with a grin that could've been forged from pure mischief.

"Here's your paper, sir," Bucky announced with a tone that suggested he was more amused than apologetic.

Sheriff Royals, still reeling from the surprise, muttered, "Scared the bah-Jesus out of me, son," as he took the newspaper, his voice a mix of irritation and bewilderment.

Bucky chuckled devilishly, sporting a t-shirt that did little to hide his skinny frame. "Sorry. Sleeping again?" he asked with a smirk, adding, "See ya later."

With a squeal and a final burst of noise, Bucky's old car sped off into the night, leaving the sheriff to shake his head and grumble about the shenanigans of the younger generation. His attention turned to the paper's front page, where presumably more mundane concerns awaited him.

Meanwhile, down at Robert's Dock, Robert was busying himself with the practicalities of his trade. Under the soft glow of the dock's lights, he loaded bait onto his wooden workboat, the tasks of a fisherman continuing despite the hour.

After tossing Robert's paper onto the lawn, Bucky skidded to a stop upon seeing the man himself. Turning off his ancient car's engine, he exited the vehicle with the exaggerated care of someone who knew their car alarm was as reliable as a sieve. He approached Robert with the newspaper in hand.

Jack, Robert's Chesapeake Bay Retriever, let out a cheerful bark as he emerged from the wooden vessel. Robert, wiping his hands on a rag, made his way to the head of the dock to meet Bucky. They exchanged the paper for a handshake, and Jack, ever the friendly beast, wiggled his tail and nudged Bucky affectionately.

"How have you been, stinky?" Bucky asked, giving Jack a good-natured scratch behind the ears.

Robert, who had hoped Bucky would still be away at school, asked, "Thought you were still away at school?"

Bucky shrugged, "Yeah, well…"

Before Robert could say more, Jennifer's voice called out, "Bucky!"

Jack, ever eager for attention, bounded towards the voice. Bucky turned, a smile spreading across his face as he saw Jennifer—bouncing toward him with the kind of enthusiasm that only youth can muster.

"You're home!" Jennifer exclaimed, practically glowing with excitement.

Robert, less enthused by the sudden commotion, glared at his daughter. "What are you doing up?"

Ignoring her father's question, Jennifer flung herself into a hug with Bucky. The embrace lingered awkwardly, causing Robert to clear his throat and cross his arms in that particular parental way that said, 'Enough of this nonsense.'

Bucky, gently detaching himself from Jennifer, mumbled, "Well, um, I better get going or I'll never finish."

Jennifer, quick as a flash, planted a kiss on Bucky's cheek. In his haste to depart, Bucky tripped over his own feet and fell, causing Jennifer to stifle a giggle with her hand.

"I'm alright!" As he scrambled back to his car, Bucky called out, half to the world and half to himself. He drove off with a final burst of noise, leaving behind a bemused Jennifer and a somewhat impatient Robert.

Jennifer turned to her father, arms wide in a pleading gesture. "Please, Daddy?"

Ever the stoic figure, Robert looked at her, his silence a tacit reminder that the evening's events were far from over.

Chapter 8

"The Mermaid"

It was scarcely a blink since the sun had yawned awake when Robert took the helm of his sturdy wooden workboat. The Miles River stretched out before him, a ribbon of shimmering water weaving its way toward the vast expanse of the Chesapeake Bay.

Jennifer, his daughter, sat beside him, her face aglow with the kind of cheer that only spring air can inspire. Jack, the Chesapeake Bay Retriever, lounged comfortably at their feet, his tail thumping rhythmically against the boat's wooden floor as if keeping time with its steady chug.

Gentle and golden morning light danced merrily on the rippling waves, casting fleeting, silvery patterns that seemed to play tag with the boat's wake. The tranquil scene could have been lifted straight out of a storybook, though it was clear this chapter was more about the humdrum of daily life than any grand adventure.

The boat's engine sputtered to a stop as Robert maneuvered it into the Bay. With a practiced hand, he began laying out the crab line—a process as familiar to him as tying his own shoelaces. Jennifer, ever the spirited teenager, wasted no time in shedding her outer layers, revealing a swimsuit that, for all its bravery, was woefully out of place in the crisp morning air.

"It's a bit chilly for that, don't you think?" Robert called over, eyeing her with paternal concern and mild exasperation.

Jennifer, not one to be deterred by a mere drop in temperature, flashed him a grin. "Maybe if I was your age," she retorted with a wink as if the chill were a mere trifle in the face of youthful vigor.

Robert's brow furrowed in bemused confusion. "What does that mean?"

Jennifer laughed, a sound like ringing bells, and with a determined splash, she plunged into the water, leaving a swirl of bubbles in her wake. The cold water seemed to greet her with a hearty embrace as she swam away from the boat, her form cutting through the morning mist with effortless grace.

Robert watched her with a mixture of disbelief and resignation. His skepticism about the swim's prudence was evident, though he turned his attention away from the water's edge as the approaching hum of another workboat grew louder.

Sydney McCullan's workboat, a relic of the sea with its well-worn wood and a perpetual trail of pipe smoke, glided towards Robert's vessel. Sydney, an elderly seafarer whose face bore the weathered lines of countless sea-bound days, piloted his boat with the nonchalance of one who knew the waters better than the back of his hand. His pipe, always ready, provided a steady stream of smoke that curled lazily into the air. He waved to Robert with a familiarity born of years spent on the same stretch of water.

"Top of the morning to ya!" Sydney's voice was as gruff as the sea, yet carried an undercurrent of warmth.

Robert waved back, his own greeting muffled by a mixture of annoyance and amusement. "I thought I smelled something funny," he called out, a smirk tugging at his lips.

Sydney chuckled as he maneuvered his boat alongside Robert's, shutting off the engine with a practiced wrist flick. "It's in my Will, young lad, that you can use my flesh for bait once the Lord's through with me here."

Robert raised an eyebrow. "Nobody wants dead crabs to cook...so what good would that do me?"

Jack, ever the enthusiast, barked excitedly, his tail a blur as Sydney tossed him a bone.

Sydney's eyes twinkled with mischief as he observed Jack's delight.

"You spoil him with that stuff," Robert remarked, shaking his head.

Sydney, whose gaze had drifted towards Jennifer, now swimming with abandon in the cold water, commented, "Looks like you have yourself a mermaid in the making."

Robert glanced over at his daughter, who was submerged except for her dangling feet. "Nothing stops that girl from getting in the water," he said resignedly.

Sydney's gaze softened as he spoke of days long past. "Yeah. A lot like you when your father worked the waters."

Robert looked down, lost in thought.

Sydney continued, almost to himself, "Miss that son of a bitch bastard. The only man I met who could drink me under the table."

The mention of Robert's father drew a reflective silence, broken only by the distant murmur of the Bay.

Sydney's voice grew somber. "Some of the boys are upset. Seems the crabs are thin this season."

Robert frowned. "Without talk like that, we couldn't get a decent price for them."

Sydney shook his head, his expression grim. "No, this isn't just talk this season. They seem to think something is very wrong."

He reached into his jacket, pulling out a flask with a smooth, practiced motion. "Want a swig?"

Robert declined with a polite shake of his head. Sydney took a long pull from the flask, replacing it with a satisfying clink and re-sticking his pipe between his teeth.

"Some say this Bay is all fished up. Others are crying pollution, nitrogen..." Sydney paused, his gaze lingering on the water. "... some even think it could be Chessie."

Robert chuckled, though the sound was tinged with skepticism. "You don't believe in Chessie, do you?"

Sydney's eyes, sharp as ever, met Robert's with a knowing twinkle. "See you tomorrow, young man!"

With that, Sydney started his boat and drifted away, his laughter mingling with the sound of the waves.

Robert tossed him his boat's line, watching as Sydney's boat gradually receded into the distance.

Jennifer's voice, bright and cheerful, cut through the quiet. "Hey,

Dad?"

Robert turned to see his daughter bobbing in the water, her smile as bright as the morning sun. He scratched his head, trying to reconcile her enthusiasm with the chilly reality of the Bay.

Jack, ever the faithful companion, barked energetically, adding to the morning's chorus. Jennifer's voice came again, slightly plaintive. "Can Jack come in the water, too?"

Robert glanced at his daughter and then at the now-distant figure of Sydney. "Why don't you get back in the boat, sweetie?" he suggested his tone a mix of affection and practicality.

"But, Dad—"

"Come on, before you get sick," Robert interjected, his concern outweighing her protests.

Jennifer, though reluctant, allowed her father to pull her from the water and onto the boat. As she dried off, Robert scanned the Bay, his thoughts a turbulent blend of work, weather, and whispered legends.

Later, as the boat returned to Saint Michaels Harbor, the day's activities unfolded with a calm, familiar rhythm.

Now contented, Jennifer and Jack sat on the bow, their eyes bright with the satisfaction of a well-spent day.

Jennifer's thoughts, filled her head. about her mother and father and what memories of life in New York City she could conjur. How those juxtaposed with the beauty now surrounding her. She repondered from the conversations with others that her father became a very successful corporate lawyer. Giving that all up when her mother died to raise her back home, in St. Michaels where it was safer.

The boat glided up to the dock at Robert's house. Jack and Jennifer leaped onto the dock, sprinting across the lawn and disappearing into the house.

Meanwhile, Robert backed the boat into its slip and turned toward The Crab Claw Restaurant across the harbor. Craig, a stout man in his thirties, awaited him with a handcart.

"How did you do today, Mr. Williams?" Craig asked, his voice imbued with the casual familiarity of a local tradesman.

"I have three bushels for you today," Robert replied, handing over the baskets of live crabs.

Craig's eyes widened in surprise. "Three? That's more than all the others combined."

"Really?" Robert's surprise mirrored Craig's.

Craig began stacking the baskets, preparing them for transport. "Yeah, the old-timers are all worked up in a knot."

"That's what I hear," Robert responded, his gaze drifting to Bill Jones, the restaurant owner, who waved at him from the shadows with a bright smile.

"How's Bill doing?" Robert called out.

"Better since he started drinking again," Craig answered with a chuckle, handing Robert a wad of cash.

"Thank you, sir!" Robert said, tucking the money away.

"Thank you!" Craig echoed, disappearing into the restaurant's shadows as Robert's boat pulled away from the dock.

Steering his boat back home, Robert reflected on the morning's events and the whispered legends of the Bay, his thoughts as deep and shifting as the waters he traversed.

Chapter 9

"Daydream"

In the heart of the Chesapeake Bay, beneath a quilt of rippling water, beams of sunlight sliced through the blue depths. The scene's serenity was rudely interrupted by the splash of Jack, who leaped into the cool embrace of the water with all the enthusiasm of a dog in his element. Following his lead, Jennifer plunged in with an exuberant splash of her own, sending a storm of tiny bubbles dancing around them in a shimmering cloud.

Jack paddled with determined strokes, his paws sending gentle waves as he waded through the water, searching for Jennifer, who had slipped beneath the surface. Ever the trickster, Jennifer had ducked below to hide from her four-legged friend. She glanced up and saw Jack's head bobbing just above the water, his keen eyes scanning in every direction but hers. Quietly, she swam away from his line of sight, moving with the stealth of a practiced swimmer.

Jack, growing increasingly anxious, swam in erratic circles, his whimpers punctuating the otherwise peaceful sounds of the Bay. Jennifer surfaced slowly, finding a moment to herself, clearing her eyes of the stinging water. She looked around, expecting to see Jack's familiar face, but instead found only the vast expanse of water. The silence was palpable, and Jennifer's heart began to beat a little faster.

"Jack?" she called out, her voice trembling slightly.

When there was no response, she turned her head, the uneasy

feeling in her chest growing stronger. "Dad?" She tried again, but the quiet of the Bay swallowed her call.

The water around her shifted. Something, or someone, was moving beneath the surface, approaching her with a slow, deliberate glide. Jennifer's gaze snapped downward, and her breath caught in her throat as she saw a massive, menacing shape emerging from the depths. The fractured beams of sunlight illuminated the creature's gigantic jaws, lined with rows of razor-sharp teeth. Its eyes gleamed with a hunger that made Jennifer freeze, unable to tear her eyes away from the horrific sight.

The scene shattered like a pane of glass as Jennifer jolted upright in her desk, her scream slicing through the hum of the classroom. Her heart raced, and the remnants of her nightmare clung to her like a cold sweat. The sudden return to reality was harsh and unforgiving.

Mrs. Richardson's face loomed large before her, the stern expression betraying no sympathy for the girl's distress. "Jennifer!" Mrs. Richardson's voice was sharp, cutting through the disoriented fog of Jennifer's mind.

The rest of the class, having been jolted from their own slumbers by the commotion, burst into laughter. Jennifer's cheeks flushed a deep crimson, her embarrassment all too palpable.

"Sorry, Mrs. Richardson," Jennifer mumbled, her voice barely above a whisper.

Mrs. Richardson's eyes narrowed, her patience wearing thin. "Perhaps I need to call your father and ask him what I must do to keep you awake in this class?"

Jennifer couldn't muster a response, her face now a canvas of mortification. As the bell rang, signaling the end of the period, the other students began to rise, eager to escape the confines of the classroom.

Mrs. Richardson, clearly unamused, gave her final instructions. "I want everyone to read about the War of 1812 tonight and be ready to discuss it tomorrow."

The students shuffled out, their voices a distant murmur as Jennifer slowly gathered her scattered belongings. Mrs. Richardson sat at her desk, resuming her paperwork with a practiced air of authority.

Jennifer approached her teacher, a look of sincere contrition etched on her face. "I'm sorry, Mrs. Richardson. It won't happen again."

Mrs. Richardson's gaze remained firm, though a flicker of understanding softened her tone. "This is the fourth time you've decided to use my class as your nap time this quarter."

Jennifer's eyes dropped to the floor, the weight of her actions settling heavily on her shoulders. "It's my fault. I helped my father this morning, and..."

Mrs. Richardson cut her off, though her voice held a note of weary resignation. "You can help your father by doing what you are supposed to do."

Jennifer nodded her expression one of genuine remorse.

"Don't let it happen again," Mrs. Richardson added, her tone softening slightly.

Jennifer's face brightened with gratitude. "Thank you, Mrs. Richardson."

"Now go home, study, and then get some sleep," Mrs. Richardson instructed, returning to her paperwork.

"I will!" Jennifer promised, her voice brightening as she turned to leave.

With a skip in her step that belied her earlier discomfort, Jennifer exited the classroom, the hallways bustling with students. Despite its rocky start, the day seemed a little brighter as she headed towards the promise of home and a new evening.

Chapter 10

"Home Maker"

The sun hung low in the sky, casting a warm, golden hue upon the quaint streets of Saint Michaels. The town had a way of whispering its history to those who wandered its narrow lanes, with each brick and beam telling tales of days long past.

Jennifer, a girl of tender years but an old soul by nature, ambled along, her slender fingers guiding a stick along the pickets of a white fence. The rhythmic tapping, a gentle accompaniment to the evening birdsong, seemed to play in time with the memories that flitted through her mind.

The houses, each a testament to the colonial spirit, stood proudly in the glow of the setting sun, their weathered facades softened by the light.

Jennifer rounded a familiar corner, her steps slowing as she crossed the front lawn of the place she called home. The door, never locked, swung open with the ease of a well-worn path.

Upon entering the modest living room, Jennifer found her father, Robert, in a state of peaceful repose upon the old couch, a newspaper draped carelessly across his chest as if the world's weight had momentarily been lifted from his shoulders. Jack, the faithful hound, lay at his feet, his tail wagging lazily in affection as his eyes met Jennifer's.

She took in the scene, a faint smile playing on her lips as she gently replaced the newspaper with a blanket woven with care and love. In these moments, there was a quiet comfort in the small acts that defined her role as the household keeper.

The piano in the corner, a relic of happier times, stood silent witness to her daily routines. Jennifer set down her school bag beside it, her thoughts lingering for just a moment on the past before she moved toward the kitchen, where the evening meal awaited her attention.

The cool air from the refrigerator greeted her as she opened its door, the light inside casting a soft glow on the contents. She retrieved a plate of cold chicken, the remnants of a previous meal, with practiced hands before closing the door with a quiet thud.

As the evening shadows lengthened, Robert found his way to the kitchen, drawn by the promise of supper. He took a bite of the fried chicken, his eyes drifting into the distance as if searching for something lost in the years gone by.

"There are times when I catch him staring off like that," Jennifer thought, her heart aching for the sorrow she knew still lingered in his soul. She knew his thoughts often traveled back to her mother, the woman whose absence was a constant presence in their lives.

"How is it?" she asked aloud, her voice breaking the silence.

Robert looked up, a smile tugging at the corners of his mouth. "Your mother and I once had a private chef back in New York," he began, his voice tinged with the nostalgia of a life that seemed like another lifetime.

"In New York?" Jennifer echoed; her curiosity piqued.
"Yes, when you were about three, I guess," Robert continued, his

mind drifting back to the grand city and the days when life was full of promise and possibilities. "Everything that chef created was a masterpiece, but whenever he asked your mother how it was, she'd just say, 'Pretty good.'"

Jennifer's brow furrowed in disbelief. "Pretty good! Why wouldn't she say it was perfect?"

Robert chuckled softly, a sound that was both sad and sweet. "She feared that if she called it perfect, he'd stop trying to improve it."

A smile spread across Jennifer's face as she absorbed the wisdom in her father's words. "I'll keep trying," she said, her voice firm with determination.

Robert reached out and patted her hand. "Well, then it's perfect, sweetie."

At that moment, a sharp knock at the door interrupted the tender exchange, and Jack sprang to his feet, barking loudly.

"Quiet, Jack!" Robert commanded, though his voice held no real threat.

Jennifer shrugged, wiping her mouth with a napkin as she rose. "I'll get it," she offered.

But Robert waved her back. "No, stay put," he instructed, approaching the door.

Curiosity getting the better of her, Jennifer followed a few steps behind, careful not to make a sound. Her heart pounded with anticipation of who might be waiting on the other side.

Chapter 11

"The Bannisters"

The front porch of Robert's home was as inviting as ever, a place where time seemed to slow down, where the worries of the day could be set aside, even if only for a spell. The golden light of the early evening bathed the porch in a soft glow, and the creak of the old boards beneath a man's weight was a familiar sound that spoke of years gone by.

Sydney McCullan stood there, a man who had seen his fair share of life's ups and downs, his pipe puffing away like a small locomotive as he waited for Robert. The door swung open with a gentle squeak, and there stood Robert with a look of mild surprise.

"Sorry to bother you, Rob," Sydney began, his voice carrying the weight of both apology and purpose.

Robert, always quick to set aside his comfort for the sake of others, offered with a slight smile, "That's okay, Sydney. Would you like to join us for dinner?"

Sydney shook his head, a polite refusal that was as much a part of him as the hat he never left the house without. "Oh, no, thank you, son. I'm letting you know that the Bannister boy lost his boat today."

Robert's brow furrowed with concern. "Is he okay?"

"Oh no. Nothin' like that. Oh Lord, no," Sydney replied, waving off the notion with a puff of smoke. "He thought it was stolen, but it turned up scuttled on the Miles."

Robert's concern deepened. "That's the…"

"…third one this month," Sydney finished, nodding gravely.

Without hesitating, Robert returned to the house, grabbing his coat from the hook by the door. "I'll be back home a little later, sweetie," he called to Jennifer over his shoulder, his voice warm with fatherly affection. "Dinner was great!"

Jennifer watched her father leave, a slight frown tugging at her lips as she reflected on his role in the community.

Robert is the President of the Talbot County Waterman Association. Whenever something goes wrong, he is there for them to try and help.

The pair made their way to Daniel Bannister's house, a place as old and worn as the man who lived there. The Sheriff's car was already parked in the driveway, a sure sign that the situation was being taken seriously. As Robert and Sydney approached the front door, they couldn't help but notice the sign hanging by the doorbell, proclaiming, "Smith and Wesson protect this house."

Sydney tried the doorbell, but it seemed as tired as the house itself, refusing to give any sign of life. He was about to knock when a voice called from the backyard, "We're out back!"

The two men exchanged a glance before carefully making their way around the house, taking care not to trip over the assortment of old boat parts strewn about the yard.

There, amid the clutter, stood Daniel Bannister, a man who looked every bit his age and then some. He was smoking a cigarette, his face a mask of frustration, while his son, Scotty, continued to give Sheriff Royals his report.

"We found it nearly under on the Miles," Scotty said, his voice tinged with anger and disbelief. "I told my father to stop feeding that thing."

Robert and Sydney headed straight for the recovered wooden vessel, sitting high on a boat trailer. The boat had seen better days, and a large, gaping hole in the bottom stern side told its own tale.

"Shark?" Robert asked, eyeing the damage.

Sydney, ever the man of few words, shook his head. "Nope."

Robert frowned. "What then?"

Sydney just smiled, a knowing look in his eyes, but offered no further explanation. Robert rolled his eyes, not in the mood for riddles, and walked over to where the Sheriff was standing.

"What thing?" Robert asked Scotty, his tone one of genuine curiosity.

Scotty didn't hesitate. "Chessie."

At the mention of the name, Sheriff Royals cast a wary glance at Robert, who raised an eyebrow in surprise. "You think Chessie did this?"

Scotty nodded, his conviction clear. "I know it did. My father keeps feeding her from my boat on my days off. The damn thing was looking for more freebies, I guess."

Sensing the conversation was getting away from him, Daniel chimed in defensively. "I didn't feed that thing. Well, I did, but ah, not that much."

"You have to, Daddy," Scotty shot back, his frustration bubbling.

Daniel shrugged, looking sheepish. "Not a lot…"

"And how much exactly is a lot to you?" Scotty pressed, his patience wearing thin.

Leaving the Bannisters to their argument, Robert, Sydney, and Sheriff Royals stepped aside for a private conference.

"What do you think?" Robert asked the Sheriff, his voice low. "Shark?"

Sydney shook his head again, his pipe puffing away.

Sheriff Royals, ever the voice of reason, considered the possibility. "Not likely a shark would come this far up the river. Bull shark, I guess, is possible."

"Then what else could it be?" Robert asked, his mind racing through the possibilities.

The Sheriff sighed. "These old watermen believe it to be their sea monster. It may have come loose and hit a rock…or maybe some kids messed with it…I'll get to the bottom of this."

As if on cue, a scream echoed from inside the house. "Damn it, Daniel!" came the voice of Mrs. Bannister, Daniel's elderly mother, as she appeared in the doorway, her flowery dress a stark contrast to the scene unfolding in the yard.

Despite her years, she had the air of a woman who had seen it all and wasn't about to put up with nonsense.

"I just saw another rat…set those traps and spread that poison as I told you to two days ago!" she barked, her tone leaving no room for argument.

"Yes, Mama," Daniel muttered, waving to his guests before hurrying inside to meet his mother's demands.

Scotty walked over to Robert and the others, his face flushed with embarrassment. "Sorry about all of this," he mumbled.

Sheriff Royals offered a reassuring nod. "Me too, son. We'll do what we can to get to the bottom of this. Let us know if we can help."

And with that, the men stood silently for a moment, the weight of the situation settling in. The evening air was thick with the scent of saltwater and pipe smoke, and somewhere in the distance, the river lapped gently against the shore as if mocking the chaos that had just unfolded.

Chapter 12

"The Siren"

It was in the wee small hours of the morning, the kind of time when most respectable folk are snug in their beds, that the familiar bark of Jack, the ever-faithful dog broke the tranquility of Robert's front yard. Jack was drawn to Bucky, who was making his rounds.

"Hi, old boy," Bucky greeted, giving Jack a friendly pat. As he approached Robert, who stood by the porch in his nightgown, Bucky tipped his hat in respect. "Good morning, sir," he added.

Robert nodded curtly. "She's still inside, getting ready," he replied, his eyes scanning the dimly lit street.

With a smile, Bucky turned back towards his rickety old car. As he pressed a button on his remote, the alarm gave a tired beep and deactivated. Just then, the front door burst open, and out rushed Jennifer, barefoot and wrapped only in a towel. She dashed towards Bucky, her cheeks flushed from the chill of the night air.

"Jennifer!" Robert's voice was stern, but it was clear his daughter had no intention of listening. She continued her mad dash, one hand clutching the towel tightly around her.

"Bucky, wait!" she called out, her voice urgent.

Bucky, startled, turned to face her. Upon seeing her attire, or lack thereof, his face turned a shade of red that could rival a ripe tomato. He quickly averted his gaze, darting to anything but Jennifer or her father.

"Oh, hi," he mumbled awkwardly.

"What are you doing this Friday night?" Jennifer asked, ignoring the fact that she was still in nothing but a towel.

Bucky kept his eyes firmly on the ground. "I'd love to take you out, but I won't get paid for another week," he confessed, his embarrassment palpable.

"Jenny, get some clothes on," Robert interjected, his patience wearing thin.

Undeterred, Jennifer leaned in and kissed Bucky on the cheek. Then, with a mischievous glint in her eye, she began to back away towards the house.

"Don't worry about it... I'll pay... this time," she said, a playful smile dancing on her lips.

Bucky, still flustered, managed a shy nod. "Okay, see you at 7?"

"Okay, 7!" Jennifer confirmed before returning to the house, her towel flapping in the breeze.

Bucky watched her go, shaking his head in bemusement before climbing into his car. The old engine sputtered to life with a groan, and he continued his morning route, delivering papers to the sleepy neighborhood.

Thus ended a peculiar chapter in the quiet town's early morning, leaving Robert to ponder over the events that had just unfolded and Bucky to dream of the upcoming Friday night.

Chapter 13

"Remarkable Calling"

The Chesapeake lay in tranquil splendor beneath the morning sun, its waters shimmering like a bed of diamonds. As carefree as a young nymph, Jennifer reclined on her back, soaking up the early rays in her scanty bathing suit, her face turned skyward in blissful repose.

Nearby, Robert, her father, busied himself with the morning's catch. He upended a basket of crabs onto a weathered wooden table, the crustaceans scrambling in every direction. With the practiced hand of a seasoned fisherman, he sorted through them, tossing the small fry back into the bay to grow another day.

The sun had barely dipped below the horizon when the sleepy town of Saint Michaels found itself abuzz with unprecedented excitement. Sydney McCullan, his face weathered and eyes twinkling with a secret, stood at the helm of his modest boat, addressing Robert with a tone full of significance.

"Chessie is on everybody's brain lately," he declared, a knowing smile playing on his lips. He then revved up the engine and, with a final look, added, "You will see, young Williams. You will see!" With that, he piloted his boat away, leaving Robert to mull over his cryptic words.

Chapter 14

"The Waterman Association"

That evening, the firehouse was alive with a cacophony of voices. Watermen and their families had gathered, each eager to voice their concerns. The air was thick with tension, arms crossed and heads shaking in disbelief. Robert and Jennifer slipped in quietly from the back. Jennifer quickly found Bucky and his parents while Robert made his way to the front, where Larry from the Maryland Natural Resource Police and Sheriff Royals intercepted him.

"Hi guys, it looks like a party," Robert remarked, eyes scanning the agitated crowd.

"Try to keep this crowd under control, Robby," Sheriff Royals advised, his tone serious. "Some seem a bit worked up, and we don't want anyone to get hurt."

Larry, unable to contain himself, interjected, "Bob, you have to understand, a lot of these folks believe that Chessie is real. The State of Maryland's position—"

"Save this for when it's your turn to talk, Larry. Okay?" Robert cut him off, moving through the throng to the President's Chair at the head of a long row of fold-out tables. A large sign behind him proclaimed "Talbot County Waterman Association."

"Order, please," Robert called, banging a small gavel. Slowly, the room quieted.

"I haven't seen a crowd like this since our last beer-tasting festival," he quipped, eliciting a ripple of laughter. The Secretary began jotting down minutes in a small notebook.

"I now call for a vote to open the floor to the members. All those opposed?" Silence followed. "So be it. Who is going to start us off?"

The room erupted into a chaotic chorus of voices, each trying to outshout the other. Robert banged his gavel again. "Order. Hold it, please. One at a time."

The crowd settled, and Manny, a man with a perpetual layer of grime and a smell of the sea, stood up.

"Chessie is eating up all the crabs, Robby!" he shouted.

Another waterman, with a thick accent and rough hands, rose to his feet. "We barely have enough catch to pay fer our fuel, let alone feed our families."

Manny continued, "We want to know what the State intends to do about it!"

All eyes turned to Larry, who stepped up hesitantly. "The State of Maryland maintains that Chessie doesn't exist," he stated.

The room exploded into an uproar. Robert hammered his gavel with renewed vigor. "Please, let him say what he has to say." The crowd grudgingly quieted.

Larry took a deep breath. "We understand that the crab population is lower than normal this year. But it has to do with the environment, not some crab-eating monster."

"Bullshit!" someone shouted from the back.

Larry pressed on, "I know you and your families rely on crabbing for a living, but year after year, the signs have been telling all of us to look for something else to do to pay your bills."

A voice from the back of the room cut through the air. "They may not know how to do anything else." Heads turned to see Daniel Bannister, a burly man with a steely gaze, pushing his way through the crowd with his son, Scotty, in tow.

"I apologize for the intrusion, folks. I know I ain't a member of this or any other piece-of-shit association. But you all know nobody cares about us watermen," Daniel said, glaring at Larry. "...especially Larry. Hell, the government will pay him no matter what happens to us, he has nothing to lose. You stand up there in your pretty little uniform and look at us with your good-for-shit know-it-all attitude and flat-out call us liars."

The crowd murmured in agreement. "You're supposed to patrol the waters, Larry. You don't even bother to do that for your paycheck. I only see you sleeping in the shade of Perry Cove. Shit, you wouldn't have seen Chessie if he bit you in your ass."

Laughter rippled through the room. Larry swallowed hard, his confidence visibly shaken. Daniel turned back to the crowd. "You all came here tonight hoping to get some help from the State. Hell, they ain't going to do shit for us. We are nothing but a bunch of drunken ignorant liars to them."

The crowd roared in unison, "Yeah!"

Sydney McCullan stepped in, cutting through the fervor. "What are you going to do about it, Danny?"

Daniel's gaze fixed on Sydney. "What did you say, old man?"

The room fell silent, all eyes on Sydney. "I asked, what are you going to do about it? You know the waters as well as, if not better than, any of us. Right?"

Daniel hesitated, rubbing his stubbled chin. "Catch it?"

His son Scotty whispered something in his ear, and the crowd began to murmur in agreement. "Yeah! Catch him, Danny!" someone shouted.

Daniel glanced at Sydney, who added, "You don't have to hurt it, just catch it alive."

Daniel nodded slowly. "Catch it."

With a plan forming, Daniel's son Scotty followed him out of the room. The crowd cheered as Larry looked at Robert, shaking his head in disbelief.

Outside, the crowd dispersed into the foggy night.
Robert, Sydney, and Jennifer walked away from the firehouse.

Chapter 15

"Another Story"

"That went well," Sydney remarked.

"Oh yeah, whatever that was," Robert replied.

"You did fine, son. What do you say we top off the evening with a little Scotch?"

"No, I'm going to bed."

Sydney zigzagged towards the Carpenter Street Saloon as Robert and Jennifer passed a large gray-stone church. "Just remember, son. Even a hermit crab needs a bigger shell once in a while."

Robert waved, and Sydney returned the gesture, whistling an Irish tune as he headed to the bar. Jennifer and Robert continued walking home.

"Dad?"

"Yes?"

"Can you tell me another story about Mom?"

Robert thought for a moment. "I bought your mother this Italian sports car when we lived in New York. Twelve cylinders... the works!"

"What kind?" Jennifer interrupted.

"The problem with a car like that in the city is that they don't function very well at low speeds. The oil doesn't get to the cylinders, and occasionally, they get so hot from the friction that they melt and weld together..."

"Yeah, whatever. What happened?"

"Your mother was pregnant with you then, and she was on a little street trying to get over to Fifth Avenue."

Robert recounted the tale of Shelley, his late wife, navigating the Ferrari through New York's crowded streets, only for the engine to die at a red light, much to the chagrin of the Volkswagen driver behind her.

"She was so embarrassed," Robert concluded.

"Did you fix the car?" Jennifer asked.

"No, we sold it and got her a car better suited for the city."

Jennifer and Robert walked silently, their bond growing stronger with each shared memory.

Chapter 16

"Wake Up!"

The following morning in school, Jennifer found herself drifting into the sweet embrace of slumber. History class, with its monotone recitations of dates and battles, had lulled her into a peaceful sleep. Behind her, a mischievous classmate, seized by a fit of mischief, attempted to tie her hair to the back of her chair. As his fingers twisted the strands, Mrs. Richardson's stern voice cut through the air like a sharp knife.

"Don't even think about it," she warned, her eyes narrowing at the boy. He quickly dropped Jennifer's lock of hair and slunk back into his seat, returning to his book with feigned innocence.

Mrs. Richardson, about to rouse Jennifer from her nap, was interrupted by the sudden entrance of the principal, his face flushed with excitement.

"History is being made out at the harbor, Mrs. Richardson. Perhaps your class would like to witness it?" he announced, his voice echoing through the room. Without waiting for a response, he exited to inform the other teachers.

Mrs. Richardson clapped her hands to gain attention. "Okay, everybody, line up quickly!" The students sprang from their chairs and hurried to the door. Mrs. Richardson pointed at the boy behind Jennifer. "Wake her up!"

Jennifer groggily opened her eyes, bewildered to see her classmates entering the bustling hallway.

<h1 style="text-align:center">Chapter 17</h1>

<h2 style="text-align:center">"Chessie Does Exist!"</h2>

Meanwhile, at the harbor, trucks with satellite dishes towered into the sky, and swarms of news helicopters filled the air. The tranquil town was transformed into a hub of frenzied activity.

Robert and his trusty dog, Jack, were dozing on the living room couch when the phone rang, jolting them awake. Without hesitation, Robert grabbed his coat and rushed out, with Jack close behind. The excitement pulled them towards the harbor, where Daniel's fishing trolley was making its grand entrance.

As Robert weaved through the throng of reporters and cameramen, he caught snippets of a news reporter's broadcast, "…we just received word that the man who claims he caught the legendary sea monster, Chessie, has just entered the mouth of Saint Michaels harbor." The words sent a thrill down his spine.

Arriving at the water's edge, Robert watched in amazement as Daniel's boat dropped anchor. Music blared from the vessel, and on the bow, Scott signaled the crowd to cheer.

"Ladies and Gentlemen," Daniel's voice boomed over the PA system, "I am so glad you are here today. Today, we will show the State, and the rest of the world for that matter, that Chessie is not a myth but a real creature with a very healthy appetite."

Robert felt a tap on his shoulder. Turning, he saw Sydney McCullan, who gave him a knowing smile. "Bring her up, son!"

Daniel commanded.

Scott, perched on a small control platform, activated the crane. Slowly, it began to lift a netted creature from the depths. The crowd gasped as the net rose, revealing a writhing, squealing creature entangled within.

"Ladies and Gentlemen…meet Chessie!" Daniel announced proudly. The creature swung from the crane, its large fins flapping desperately. Cameras flashed, capturing every moment.

"That's not Chessie," Sydney muttered to Robert, who looked puzzled.

Just then, a more enormous sea creature lunged from the water, aiming to free the smaller one. "What the hell?" Daniel exclaimed, nearly losing his footing.

Sydney's eyes twinkled. "That's Chessie!" he declared, a broad smile spreading.

Daniel's surprise was palpable. "It's the damn thing's mother! Put it back down, son!" he shouted over the din. But Scott caught up in the chaos, couldn't hear him. "Cut it loose! Now!" Daniel ordered desperation in his voice.

The more enormous creature crashed back into the water, sending waves nearly tipping the vessel. Water splashed over the patrons at the Crab Claw Restaurant, causing screams and chaos.

In a panic, Scott pulled the wrong lever, only half-dropping the net. The baby creature struggled, the net tightening around its neck. The crowd watched in horror as it gasped for air. In the mother's eye, Scott saw his reflection just before she lunged, biting him in half. Pandemonium erupted as officers fired their guns at the enraged creature.

"No!" Daniel screamed, climbing the crane to cut the rope. Chessie, in a protective fury, leapt again, smashing into the dock, killing an officer and two spectators. The crowd struggled to safety as Chessie bit off the entire lower half of Daniel. With one final, heart-wrenching scream, Daniel severed the rope, and Chessie and her baby fell back into the water.

Chapter 18

"A Mother's Grief"

Beneath the now eerily quiet waters of Saint Michaels harbor, Chessie worked desperately to free her baby from the net. The creature's squeals were now soft whimpers. She pulled and tugged at the net until her baby rolled free, but it was too late. Her baby lay lifeless.

With a mournful cry, Chessie nudged her baby, but there was no response. She let out a loud, penetrating squeal that echoed through the depths, then gently pulled her lifeless offspring deeper into the murky waters, disappearing beyond light's reach.

Chapter 19

"Linda"

In the heart of New York City, where the hustle and bustle of life never seemed to sleep, there sat a bar and restaurant, humming with the evening's energy. Patrons crowded around tables, their laughter mingling with the clinking of glasses, while others stood or perched on stools at the bar, their eyes occasionally drifting to the flickering televisions overhead, each one playing a different story.

Among the din, a waiter navigated through the crowded room, carefully balancing a bottle of wine. He made his way to a table where Linda, an attractive woman of a certain age, sat with her date, George—a man who, despite his expensive suit, seemed as out of place in the casual setting as a cat in a dog show. George, however, was too engrossed in his laptop to notice the world around him, his fingers flying over the keyboard as if he were conducting a symphony of digital commerce.

The waiter, eager to do his job, presented the bottle for George's approval. But George, without so much as lifting his eyes from the screen, dismissed him with a curt, "Show it to her." His attention never wavered from the glowing screen in front of him.

Linda, accustomed to such treatment, let out a quiet sigh as the waiter turned to her with the label. She nodded in approval, and the waiter poured a small taste into her glass. Swirling the wine, she brought it to her nose, inhaled the aroma, and took a tiny sip. It was fine. Just fine.

"This is fine," she said, her voice tinged with resignation. The waiter filled her glass, then moved to George's, though his efforts went entirely unnoticed.

As the waiter retreated, Linda's eyes fell on George, who was now fully absorbed in a fierce bidding war on eBay. His focus was absolute, his face lit by the screen's glow, utterly oblivious to the world around him. Linda, feeling the weight of his neglect, let her gaze wander about the room. She noticed other couples, laughing, talking, enjoying each other's company—everything that her evening was not.

Her eyes then drifted to one of the televisions at the bar. The flickering images suddenly caught her full attention. The screen displayed scenes from Saint Michaels harbor, showing the chaos and excitement that had unfolded earlier that day. The images of Chessie, the legendary sea creature, and the turmoil surrounding its capture, captivated her.

Without a word to George, who hadn't noticed her departure, Linda made her way to the bar, where she stood, mesmerized by the unfolding drama on the screen. A man in a cowboy hat, seeing her interest, tipped his hat and offered her his stool.

"Would you like to sit, ma'am?" he asked politely.

Linda smiled, appreciating the gesture. "No, thank you," she replied, her eyes never leaving the screen.

Turning to the bartender, she asked, "Bartender?"
He approached with a friendly smile. "What can I do you for?"

"Would you please turn up the volume on the news here for a minute?" she requested.

"Certainly," the bartender replied, reaching for the remote. As the sound increased, the television exploded with images of Chessie and the aftermath of the confrontation at the harbor.

The news reporter's voice narrated the chaos: "…the animal lashed out at the local fisherman's vessel. Five are reported wounded or maimed while at least three are left dead."

Linda leaned in closer, her voice barely a whisper, "A Plesiosaur."

The bartender glanced at her curiously as the news report continued. "The historical watermen town of Saint Michaels is now holding a special meeting about how to catch and destroy the animal."

Suddenly resolute, Linda turned from the bar, her mind made up. She hurried back to her table, her steps quick and purposeful. She snatched up her purse and addressed George without bothering to wait for him to look up.

"I'm going to Maryland for a few days. I'll call you when I get back," she declared, her tone leaving no room for discussion.

Still immersed in his digital conquest, George responded with a distracted "Shhhh!" as if she were nothing more than a mild annoyance. Linda, her patience worn thin, shook her head in disbelief and walked away.

Moments later, George erupted in triumph. "Yes!!! I got it, honey!" he exclaimed, finally looking up, ready to share his victory—only to find the seat across from him empty. He glanced around, puzzled, then shrugged and buried his head back in his laptop, utterly unconcerned by her absence.

And so, the evening went on, with George content in his virtual world, unaware that Linda had stepped out of his life and into a story far more real than anything his computer screen could offer.

Chapter 20

"An Emergency Meeting"

Back in the Saint Michaels Firehouse meeting hall, the air was thick with tension as watermen, their families, and concerned citizens filled every available space. The murmur of voices fell silent as Robert, standing at the front of the room, called for attention.

"If we can all have a moment of silence for those we lost today and those that were injured," Robert began, his voice solemn and steady.

A hush fell over the room. Heads bowed, and for a brief moment, the only sound was the creaking of the old building settling into the weight of the grief it held. It was a rare moment of unity in a town divided by fear and uncertainty.

Robert cleared his throat, breaking the silence. "Okay. If we are going to kill this thing, we might as well do it in an organized manner."

Larry, clad in his official uniform, rose to address the crowd. His face was stern, but his eyes showed a hint of weariness. "The Governor's office wants this thing bagged and stuffed as soon as possible before it scares everyone away from our waters. The state is asking for our help. Now, the Coast Guard and our Natural Resource Police are combing the Bay as we speak. Many of you claim to frequently see Chessie."

There was a collective nodding of heads among the watermen,

their faces etched with a mixture of fear and determination. They had lived their lives by these waters, and now those same waters had turned against them, harboring a creature as mysterious as it was terrifying.

Larry continued, "Well, now is the time to put our differences aside and work together to make the Bay safe again."

From the back of the room, Sydney McCullan shook his head silently, his expression hard to read. He'd seen enough in his time to know that not every monster could be slain with brute force.

Sensing the unease, Robert lifted his head and addressed the crowd again. "What we are about to do may prove to be rather dangerous," he admitted, his gaze sweeping the room until it landed on Jennifer, standing quietly off the side. Her eyes met his, full of questions she hadn't dared to ask.

"I need to know how many of you will volunteer to help find this thing," Robert asked, his voice steady despite the uncertainty of what lay ahead.

Every hand in the room shot up, rough and calloused from years of labor on the water. These men and women had faced storms, droughts, and lean seasons, but nothing quite like this.

Robert nodded, taking in the concerned faces around him. "We'll meet out at the docks at 5 AM sharp. Go home and get some rest. It's going to be a long day tomorrow."

With that, Robert stood, the weight of his responsibility heavy on his shoulders, and left the room. The crowd erupted into conversation, the tension now channeled into frantic planning and speculation. Jennifer hurried after her father, her worry clear in her eyes.

Chapter 21

"A Father's Resolve"

Back at home, Robert sat hunched over his computer, the glow of the screen casting a pale light across his face. He scoured the internet, searching for stories, myths, anything that might give him an edge in understanding the creature that had turned his quiet town upside down.

Jennifer entered the room, her footsteps soft on the floorboards. For a moment, she watched him in silence, her heart heavy with the fear that had been growing all evening.

"Do you need anything else before I go to bed?" she asked, her voice barely above a whisper.

Robert didn't look up, his focus was still on the screen. "No, sweetie. I'm fine. Get some sleep."

But Jennifer didn't move. She stood in the doorway, her eyes fixed on her father, who seemed so distant despite being only a few feet away.

"Are you really going to kill Chessie, Dad?" she asked, the question finally breaking through her hesitation.

Robert paused, his fingers still on the keyboard. He looked up at her, his face softening. "That is what the people want to do. At the moment, the waters appear unsafe with her about."

Tears welled up in Jennifer's eyes, and she couldn't hold them back any longer. She crossed the room and stood beside her father, her small frame trembling with fear. Robert, sensing her distress, pulled her into a hug, holding her tightly as she cried.

"Oh, sweetie, nothing is going to change. I'll be alright," he whispered, though he wasn't entirely sure of the truth in his own words.

Jennifer buried her face in his shoulder, her voice muffled by tears. "I want to go with you, Daddy."

Robert shook his head gently, lifting her chin so she could see the firmness in his eyes. "Oh no. You are going to school. You don't want to be a part of this."

But Jennifer knew there was more to it than just school. She knew her father was trying to protect her from something far more significant than a creature in the bay. And as she reluctantly pulled away and headed to bed, she couldn't shake the feeling that the world she had known was slipping away, replaced by something darker, something more dangerous than she had ever imagined.

Chapter 22

"Assembling the Hunt"

The morning sun rose over Chesapeake Bay, casting a golden hue across the waters. The bay, usually calm and serene, was now a hive of activity. Boats dotted the surface in strategic lines, their occupants scanning the horizon with a mix of anticipation and dread. Above, helicopters buzzed like restless bees, and aircraft crisscrossed the sky, all searching for the elusive Chessie.

The atmosphere on Robert's workboat was tense. Robert and Sydney McCullan listened intently to the crackling radio transmissions that filled the air.

Jennifer, who'd fought the good fight and come out the victor, skipping school with the kind of triumph only the young can muster, sat in the back alongside their trusty dog, Jack. Their eyes, as wide as saucers, took in the grand parade of life that sprawled out before them, a spectacle unfolding with all the wonder and mischief they could have hoped for.

"A real mess if you ask me," Sydney muttered under his breath, shaking his head at the chaos.

Jennifer cleared her throat pointedly, and Sydney, catching himself, quickly added, "Sorry about that, my lady."
Robert turned to his daughter, his voice firm but gentle. "Stay there where I can see you both."

Jack, sensing the tension, whined softly and lay down, his panting the only sound in the momentary lull.

Chapter 23

"Cooling Off in Tunis Mills"

Four lively little rascals, no bigger than half-pints, stood at the edge of the old Tunis Mills Bridge, each one strapped into a life jacket that looked nearly big enough to swallow them whole. Their faces were alight with the pure, unspoiled excitement of some grand adventure just moments away.

Below, the creek meandered along, slow and lazy, its waters twinkling in the sunlight like it had not a care in the world. Their mothers, standing a few paces back, exchanged glances—half amused, half concerned—watching as their mischievous brood prepared to throw themselves headlong into the gentle embrace of the waiting water.

"Remember, no splashing!" one of the mothers called out, her voice echoing across the water. She was trying to maintain some semblance of order, though her words seemed as effective as asking the sun not to shine.

Full of energy and mischief, the children were already racing toward the swimming deck that jutted out beneath the bridge. Their laughter filled the air as they pushed and splashed each other, heedless of their mother's half-hearted warning. The river seemed to welcome their play, usually so calm and inviting.

But beneath the surface, something stirred.

Deep in the murky water, a pair of ancient eyes watched the

children's legs kicking and splashing, sending ripples through the river. The creature, long hidden from the world, was drawn by the commotion, moving silently beneath the unsuspecting swimmers.

Just as one of the children reached the deck, a massive, scaly head burst from the water with a roar that echoed like thunder. It was Chessie, the creature of legend, and her sudden appearance sent a shockwave of terror through the small group.

The children screamed, their joyful shouts turning to cries of fear as they clutched at their ears, trying to block out the deafening sound. Chessie's roar was a warning, a primal command that froze the mothers on the bridge in their tracks, their faces pale with horror.

Sensing the fear, Chessie dipped back beneath the surface, but not before creating a massive wave that surged toward the swimming deck. The children were swept up by the wave and carried closer to the safety of the shore. Their terror-stricken mothers, finally snapping out of their paralysis, screamed for them to get out of the water, their voices shrill with panic.

Amid the chaos, one of the mothers, driven by a mix of fear and anger, hurled her soda bottle at Chessie. The plastic bottle arced through the air, striking Chessie squarely on her exposed back.

The creature paused momentarily, as if in disbelief that something so small could be so bold. Then, with a swift flick of her mighty tail, she sent a sheet of water cascading over the bridge, drenching the mothers where they stood.

With that, Chessie dove beneath the surface, her powerful form slicing through the water as she raced downriver, disappearing as quickly as she had come. The river returned to its peaceful state as if nothing out of the ordinary had happened at all.

The children huddled together on the swimming deck, watching in awe and relief as the last ripples of Chessie's wake faded into the distance. Their mothers, soaked to the skin and trembling with the aftershock of terror, rushed to their sides, pulling them to safety with shaking hands.

For a moment, the only sounds were the dripping of water and the heavy breathing of those who had just faced something they could scarcely comprehend. Then, slowly, life returned to the bridge. The mothers, gathering their wits, exchanged looks of disbelief while the wide-eyed children clung to them, their earlier bravado completely forgotten.

The legend of Chessie had just become very real, and no one on that bridge would ever forget the day they came face to face with the creature of the deep.

Chapter 24

"Don't Shoot!"

Robert's radio erupted with frantic chatter.

"Manny's got something!" came the voice over the speaker, full of urgency.

Robert, quickly snapping back to the task at hand, grabbed the microphone. "Where are you, Manny?"

"At the mouth of Leeds Creek," Manny's voice crackled through the speaker, excitement barely contained.

"We're on our way," Robert replied, steering the boat toward Manny's location.

Sydney grinned, the thrill of the chase lighting up his eyes. "This is where the fun starts."

Jennifer clung to Jack as the boat roared to life, cutting through the water with purpose.

As they neared the scene, Robert slowed his boat, allowing Larry's patrol boat to take the lead. In the distance, Chessie's massive head broke the surface, letting out a ferocious roar before thrashing her tail violently, sending waves crashing into the surrounding boats. Robert's boat pulled alongside Larry's, the tension thick as they took in the sight of the creature surrounded by 15 workboats, each one a tiny island in a sea of danger.

"I'll be damned. We got her now," Larry muttered, his hand tightening on his rifle. "Hang on, in case she gets violent."

Jennifer, unable to bear the sight, closed her eyes and covered her ears. "I can't watch this."

"Might as well do what we came to do," Larry said, his voice grim.

"Shoot her, Larry, shoot her!" Manny's voice urged from a nearby boat.

Larry took aim, his finger hovering over the trigger. The sound of the gunshot echoed across the water, and Robert's heart sank as the bullet found its mark, nicking the back of Chessie's neck and drawing blood. Chessie's eyes widened with pain and fury, and she thrashed about in the water, her roars filling the bay.

As Larry reloaded his rifle, a siren wailed from a nearby boat. Just as Larry was about to fire again, Robert acted on instinct, deflecting the rifle just in time to prevent another shot. A new boat was seconds away from the line of fire.

Chessie, now bleeding and enraged, smashed into the net that had ensnared her. The force of her movements sent the surrounding boats rocking like toys in a bathtub. The men on board struggled to keep their balance as Chessie leapt over the new boat, landing between Larry's and Manny's with a splash that drenched them all.

But before Larry could react, Chessie made her move, racing toward freedom, her powerful tail sending waves crashing into the boats.

"Damn!" Larry cursed, grabbing the radio. "Is everyone okay?"

One by one, the boats reported back, each crew shaken but unharmed. All eyes then turned to the uninvited boat, where Dr. Linda Olson stood, watching as Chessie fled to safety.

"What in the heck are you trying to do, get yourself killed?" Larry shouted across the water.

Linda, unflinching, replied, "My name is Dr. Linda Olson, and I'm from the National Oceanic Association. I'm here to stop you from killing that animal."

Larry, exasperated, tried to assert his authority. "Listen, Ms. Olson—"

"Dr. Olson," she corrected, her voice firm.

"Dr. Olson, we have orders from the Governor of Maryland to have that animal on his barbecue grill by dinner time," Larry retorted, his patience wearing thin.

"Not if I have anything to say about it. That 'monster' you call Chessie happens to be a Plesiosaur" Linda shot back.

"A what?" Larry asked, bewildered.

"A Plesiosaur, a dinosaur thought to be extinct. We need it alive," Linda explained as she spun her boat around, preparing to follow Chessie.

"Call off the hunt before the world discovers just how ignorant all of you are!" she added, her voice carrying a note of finality as her boat sped off in the last known direction of Chessie.

As the roar of her engine faded into the distance, Sydney couldn't help but chuckle. "Feisty little thing, isn't she?"

Still processing the encounter, Robert couldn't take his eyes off Linda. Jennifer noticed her father's gaze and wondered how this unexpected turn would change their lives.

Chapter 25

"Change of Plan"

On that warm summer night, the front porch of Robert Williams' home was a gathering place for troubled souls. A small crowd of watermen had assembled, their faces shadowed by the flickering lanterns that dotted the porch. The air was thick with tension, and questions hung like storm clouds.

"What in God's name is going on, Rob?" asked one of the watermen, his voice tinged with frustration. Others murmured their agreement, echoing the sentiment. Jennifer clutched Jack, her loyal dog, as he panted nervously in her arms. Sydney McCullan leaned against a post, quietly observing the crowd from his place behind Robert.

Robert, ever the steady presence, waited calmly for the noise to subside. When, at last, the murmurs died down, he cleared his throat and addressed the anxious faces before him. "Folks, if you could give me a moment…" He reached into a cardboard overnight envelope and withdrew a document, unfolding it deliberately as the crowd watched in tense silence.

"We aren't on a hunt anymore," Robert announced, his voice cutting through the night air.

The crowd reacted with a mix of confusion and disbelief, but no one interrupted. Robert continued, "We are now on a rescue mission."

A ripple of incredulity swept through the group. "What in the hell does that mean?" one of the watermen blurted out, his voice rising with agitation.

Robert held up the document. "I have here a fax from the Governor's Office ordering us to cease and desist all plans of killing the Plesiosaur we all know as Chessie. The message is clear: Chessie is to be caught, but not harmed in any way."

A few men in the crowd cursed under their breath. Manny, always quick to speak his mind, muttered, "That son of a bitch."

Another waterman voiced what many were thinking, "That just figures!"

But Robert pressed on, trying to keep the situation under control. "It isn't just him. The President of the United States has given the order."

"Damn the President!" shouted a voice from the crowd, and others cheered in agreement, their anger palpable.

Robert raised his hand for silence, continuing with the grim news. "Chessie is now a federally protected animal. Anyone who attempts to harm her will face five years in prison and a $500,000 fine."

The crowd's disbelief was almost tangible. They had expected a fight, not a legal battle. Robert softened his tone as he added, "Each member of a team that manages to capture Chessie alive will receive a $50,000 reward."

As the men digested this, Mrs. Bannister, an elderly woman who had seen more than her share of sorrow, made her way to the front of the crowd. Her eyes were tired, red from the tears she had shed over the past few days. When she spoke, her voice was soft, but it carried the weight of her grief.

"You mean we're not going to kill it?" she asked, her gaze fixed on Robert.

The crowd fell silent, all eyes on Robert as he struggled to find the right words. But before he could respond,

Mrs. Bannister continued, her voice breaking. "My grandson is dead, Mr. Williams. My son's legs were bitten off by that… that beast! He's lucky to be alive. What about the families of those who weren't so lucky? What about the others that were killed? Is this their reward?"

She couldn't hold back her tears any longer. As they streamed down her face, she glanced at Jennifer, the weight of her words heavy in the air. "Imagine if it was your little girl."

Robert was left speechless, his heart aching for the pain she had endured. Mrs. Bannister turned away, her sobs muffled as she disappeared into the crowd, which parted for her with a quiet reverence.

"I know this isn't what we expected to hear," Robert finally said, his voice somber. "As your representative, it's my duty to let you know what the rules are."

But no one was in the mood for rules. "It sounds like a bunch of horseshit to me," muttered a man from the back, and the crowd grumbled in agreement.

Robert stood firm. "Those who want to join the rescue mission can meet me at the marina tomorrow morning at 5:00 AM."

With that, the crowd began to disperse, breaking into small groups that murmured amongst themselves as they melted into the darkness of the night. Sydney stepped up beside Robert, watching the men leave. He gave Robert a pat on the back, a gesture of solidarity.

"I wouldn't count on too much help, son," Sydney said, his tone laced with the wisdom of experience.

Robert nodded, a hint of resignation in his eyes. "I know."

Jennifer called Jack into the house, and the dog obediently trotted inside. Sydney started to walk away, but then paused and turned back to Robert.

"Care for a swig of Scotch? It might do you some good."

Robert shook his head. "No, I should get some sleep."

Sydney tipped his hat. "See you in the morning, if the morning should come."

"Thanks, Syd. Good night."

Robert watched Sydney disappear into the night before making his way around to the back of the house. He followed the dock out over the water, which sparkled in the moonlight, and stood there for a long while, lost in thought as the beauty of the scene failed to ease the burden on his heart.

Chapter 26

"Robert's Home"

The following day, Robert and Jack were on the boat, slowly making their way across the harbor. Sydney's boat pulled up alongside them, Sydney at the helm, his eyes twinkling with his usual good humor.

"Top of the morning to ya," Sydney called out, reaching into his pocket for Jack's treat.

Robert chuckled. "Can't you Irish come up with anything normal to say?"

Sydney tossed the snack to Jack, who caught it eagerly and gulped it down. Sydney grinned. "If it's normal, why say it?"

Robert looked around at the few boats assembling in the harbor, concern deepening the lines on his face. "Where is everybody else?"

Sydney's expression grew more serious. "Either out crabbing or hunting."

"That's all I needed to hear," Robert said quietly, his concern shifting to resolve.

Sydney nodded toward the water. "Doesn't look like that's all you're going to hear."

Larry's Natural Resource Police boat approached, gliding up next to Robert and Sydney's boats. Larry shut off the engines and called out, "Hi guys. Where is everybody?"

Sydney's voice took on a sarcastic edge as he replied, "I guess that lady biologist ate 'em all."

Robert and Sydney exchanged a small laugh, but Larry's face grew pale. From the lower deck of Larry's boat, Linda Olson popped her head up, holding a nautical chart in her hands, a pen clamped between her teeth. She removed the pen, her eyes locking onto Sydney with a steady gaze.

Sydney puffed on his pipe a bit more quickly, trying to steady himself under her scrutiny.

"Are you Dr. Robert Williams?" Linda asked, her voice cutting through the tension.

Sydney pointed to Robert. "I am," Robert answered.

"I'm Dr. Olson from the National Oceanic Administration," she began, but Robert finished for her.

"We kind of met yesterday."

Linda scanned the nearly empty harbor, her brow furrowing with concern. "I expected more people here to help."

Sydney dropped his gaze to the water, his head twitching nervously. Robert looked back at Linda, afraid to voice what they both knew.

"You don't believe they're still hunting her, do you?" Linda asked, her voice trembling with a mixture of disbelief and fear.

No one answered, but the silence was telling.

"They are aware that the animal is now federally protected, aren't they?" Linda pressed.

Sydney finally spoke, his voice low. "I'm afraid that doesn't concern them too much."

Linda's face flushed with anger. "That's just perfect!" she exclaimed, pacing back and forth on Larry's boat. "This is a Plesiosaur, maybe one of a few thought to be extinct. What in the world are they doing? God!"

She banged her fists on her thighs, frustration boiling over as she spun around, her hands covering her face.

Robert watched her with a mixture of admiration and concern. Sydney, sensing Robert's thoughts, simply said, "To them, it's a killer."

Linda stopped her frantic pacing, taking a deep breath. Larry, ever the pragmatist, spoke up, "One thing's for certain, we aren't going to catch it if we don't find it first."

The morning sun rose higher, casting a golden glow on the waters of the bay. As the boats prepared for what was to come, the storm clouds on the horizon loomed ever closer, a reminder that nature's fury—and Chessie's—were never far away.

Chapter 27

" Love Point "

In the tight confines of a Natural Resource Police floatplane, Sammy, the middle-aged pilot, squinted at the horizon, his experienced eyes catching the dark line creeping across the sky. He reached for the radio, his voice crackling through the static, "Larry, we got a line of thunderstorms moving in from the west."

Down below, aboard Larry's patrol boat, the message was received with furrowed brows. The boat rocked gently in the bay, where Robert, Sydney, Larry, and Dr. Linda Olson were all on edge, their binoculars sweeping the choppy waters in search of the elusive Chessie.

Sammy's voice crackled over the radio again, this time more urgent, "I have to land until it blows over."

Larry grabbed the microphone, but before he could speak, Linda's frustration boiled over. "That's just great! We'll never find her now!" she exclaimed, throwing her hands up in exasperation.

Larry waited for her to finish before calmly responding to Sammy, "Okay, Sammy. We'll see you later. Thanks for your help."

Above Chesapeake Bay, Sammy circled once more, his plane dipping low over Larry's boat as he offered a final, "Good luck and be safe," before banking away toward the safety of land.

Larry sighed as he watched the plane fade into the distance, the dark clouds looming ever closer. "I guess we better call it a night," he said, his voice heavy with resignation. "It'll be dark before we get back."

Linda, her face flushed with anger, dropped into a seat, crossing her arms like a child denied her favorite toy. She huffed and puffed, her frustration palpable. Sydney, ever the practical one, nodded in agreement with Larry. "I don't want to get caught out here in a storm, that's for sure."

Larry tried to reassure her, though his own disappointment was evident. "We'll try again tomorrow, Dr. Olson."

Linda managed a thin smile, though it barely masked her disappointment. Larry, ever the professional, turned back to the radio. "This is the Natural Resource Police. Due to the approaching storm, the search operation is suspended until tomorrow. Get home safely, everyone."

Meanwhile, on another part of the bay, Manny, perched on his own boat, rocked in the growing waves. He adjusted his binoculars, peering through the darkening sky at a massive object half-submerged near the shore. The wind picked up, whipping the waves into a frenzy, but Manny's focus was unwavering. A flash of lightning illuminated the object—a dark, hulking shape that could only be Chessie.

Larry's voice came over Manny's radio, but he was too transfixed by what he saw to pay attention. His engine idled as he slowly moved closer, the object growing clearer with each flash of lightning.

"This is Fish Food II calling the Natural Resource Police. Do you copy?" Manny's voice was thick with excitement and fear as he finally reached for his microphone.

Back on Larry's patrol boat, the radio crackled to life again, Larry's brow furrowing as he picked up the microphone. "We read you, but barely. Are you okay?"

Manny's voice, distorted by the storm, came through with an urgent message, "I think we found it! I think we found it!"

Robert and Linda exchanged looks, both moving closer to the radio, anticipation buzzing in the air.

"Found what?" Larry asked, his voice sharp.

Linda leaned in, unable to contain her eagerness. "Found what?"

Robert, sensing the moment's gravity, shushed her gently.

"Chessie?" Linda whispered, the word hanging in the air like a prayer.

On Manny's boat, the storm winds battered the sides as he approached the dark shape cautiously. With trembling hands, he lifted the microphone once more. "Chessie! I found Chessie!"

Back on Larry's patrol boat, Larry's mouth dropped open in shock. Linda jumped up, her excitement almost childlike, while Robert allowed himself a rare grin.

Sydney, however, kept a wary eye on the horizon, where the storm was brewing with menacing intent.

"Lord help us now," Sydney muttered under his breath, his voice almost lost in the growing wind.

Larry quickly responded to Manny, "Where are you?"

"Love Point. It's beached," came Manny's reply, the words sending a shiver through everyone on board.

"Beached?" Linda echoed, her face draining of color as she realized the implications.

A heavy silence fell over the boat, broken only by the distant rumble of thunder. "She's probably trying to kill herself. We have to get to her now," Linda urged, her voice rising with desperation.

Robert looked to Larry, seeking his judgment. Larry's gaze shifted between the approaching storm and the dark waters ahead. "We might kill ourselves too, trying to get over there in this mess," he said, his voice full of the gravity of their situation.

"What do you want me to do? I can't catch this thing alone," Manny's voice pleaded over the radio.

Linda, refusing to be deterred, clenched her fists. "We have to save her. It's just a little rain!"

A sudden flash of lightning split the sky, followed by a deafening clap of thunder that made everyone jump. Linda, undeterred, flashed a determined smile at Larry, her resolve unshaken.

Manny's voice crackled through the radio once more, desperate and insistent. "I ain't staying in this mess by myself. What do you want me to do? Over."

Robert, seeing the determination in Linda's eyes, picked up the microphone. "Stay put, Manny. We'll be right there. I'll call for another boat."

Linda, overjoyed, threw her arms around Larry in a spontaneous hug, then turned to Robert and did the same, though he stood awkwardly, unable to fully reciprocate. Sydney, ever the quiet observer, crossed himself and offered a silent prayer as the storm closed in.

Larry, shaking his head but knowing there was no turning back, turned the boat north toward Love Point. "You two better hang on. This ain't going to be fun," he warned, his voice grim as he radioed the other patrol boats.

The small police boat battled its way through the massive waves, water crashing over the sides and drenching everyone on board. Lightning flashed all around them, and thunder clapped with an intensity that rattled their bones.

Linda, focused solely on the mission, barely noticed the storm. Robert, however, was struck by the sight of her, her determination shining through even in the face of danger. He couldn't take his eyes off her, even as the wind and waves battered them from all sides. Linda, catching him staring, blushed slightly but didn't look away.

Larry, noticing the moment, rolled his eyes as he fought to keep the boat steady. It was going to be a long night, but there was no turning back now.

Chapter 28

"The Rescue"

The storm raged on, as Manny, aboard his battered boat, waved a bright flashlight through the driving rain. Three police boats, their spotlights cutting through the darkness, homed in on his location, their engines straining against the swelling waves.

On Larry's patrol boat, the beam of Manny's light pierced through the gloom. Larry, gripping the radio microphone, relayed the sighting to the other vessels. "There he is, boys. Follow me in."

Linda and Robert, huddled at the bow, strained to see through the sheets of rain. The three boats converged around Manny's, their hulls scraping the sandy point just below the storm-tossed waters.

Without a moment's hesitation, Linda leapt overboard, plunging into the icy waves, battling her way toward the hulking shadow of Chessie. Robert watched in astonishment, his heart pounding as he saw her struggle through the tumultuous water.

"What the hell is she doing?" Larry muttered, bewildered by her reckless courage. Sydney, standing steady as always, simply smiled knowingly.

Larry, ever cautious, drew his rifle, ready to defend if Chessie turned hostile. But Robert, with a firm yet gentle hand, pushed the barrel away. "Just wait," he urged, his eyes never leaving Linda as she reached the creature.

Linda, soaked to the bone, finally made contact with the ancient beast. Her trembling hand slid over Chessie's rubbery skin, and for a moment, the world seemed to stop. Tears welled in her eyes as she looked up to the stormy heavens, a smile of pure joy breaking through her exhaustion.

Robert watched from the safety of the boat, captivated by the scene unfolding before him. Sydney, noticing the admiration in Robert's gaze, smiled to himself, understanding more than he let on.

The spell was broken as Linda snapped back to reality. She turned and shouted over the howling wind, her voice urgent, "Come on! What are you doing? We have to save her!"

Spurred into action, Robert and the others jumped into the freezing water to help. Sydney remained on the boat, steadying it against the violent waves. The crew from the other boats joined in, dragging a massive net toward Chessie, hoping to coax her back into deeper water where she might find safety.

Chapter 29

"A Quiet Moment"

The night wore on, and by the time Robert returned to his kitchen, he was utterly spent. The storm had taken its toll, leaving him disheveled and weary. On the kitchen counter, a plate waited for him, covered with foil, and a note attached, written in Jennifer's neat handwriting: "HEAT IN THE MICROWAVE FOR ONE MINUTE. LOVE, JEN."

Robert smiled tiredly as he uncovered the plate and placed it in the microwave. As he waited, he noticed a soft glow emanating from the family room.

Curious, Robert entered the room to find Jennifer asleep on the couch, Jack curled at her feet. The flickering light from the television revealed that she had fallen asleep watching old home videos of her mother. A pang of nostalgia hit Robert, and he gently draped a quilt over her, not wanting to wake her from her peaceful slumber.

The microwave's beep sounded, signaling his meal was ready, but before he could move, the phone rang. Robert quickly snatched it up, answering in a hushed voice so as not to disturb Jennifer.

"Hello?" he whispered.

"Hi, it's me," came Linda's voice, warm and familiar, even through the static.

"Linda?" Robert replied, a smile tugging at his lips.

"How did you get my number?" he asked, more amused than surprised.

In her hotel room, Linda chuckled softly. "I have my ways," she teased, before quickly changing the subject. "Listen, turn the television to channel 13."

Puzzled, Robert grabbed the remote and switched the channel, turning off the home video in the process. The screen flickered to life with a news report from Baltimore, showing Linda standing near the temporary containment area where Chessie had been taken.

"It's you!" Robert exclaimed, recognizing her immediately.
"Just wait," Linda urged. "I saw the same loop earlier."

As the reporter filled the screen, Linda's voice lowered, almost conspiratorial. "Now watch in the background."

Robert leaned in, and there it was—Linda on screen, hugging and giving him a kiss. He glanced over at Jennifer, still sound asleep, and then back at the screen, a mix of emotions swirling within him.

"Our first real kiss," Linda said with a laugh, "preserved forever."

Robert couldn't help but chuckle. "You are something else, do you know that? How's your monster doing?"

Feigning mock indignation, Linda replied, "It's not a monster! She's stable, and it's so wonderful we found her."

Robert could hear the excitement in her voice, a genuine joy that was infectious. "I just can't sleep," she admitted. "I'm so excited. I owe you a nice dinner tomorrow night."

"Tomorrow night?" Robert repeated, glancing over at Jennifer, who shifted slightly in her sleep.

Linda's playful tone returned, "Auuuugh!!! Just say yes!"

"Okay, do I get to choose where?" Robert asked, amused by her persistence.

"Anywhere you wish," Linda promised.

"Hmm. Okay. I guess it's a date," Robert agreed, his smile widening.

"I'll pick you up at sixish," Linda said, her voice tinged with anticipation.

"I can't wait," Robert replied sincerely.

"Me neither," Linda said softly, and then, just before hanging up, she added with a mischievous lilt, "Robert?"

"Yes?"

"Chessie is not the only thing keeping me awake," she hinted. "Is this one of those calls?" Robert teased back, catching on.

Linda's laughter rang through the phone, light and carefree. "Maybe!"

"I'm glad I met you, Linda. Try to get some rest," Robert said, his voice full of warmth.

"Okay, you too. Goodnight," Linda replied.

"Goodnight," Robert echoed, as he hung up the phone.

For a moment, Robert stood there, staring at the receiver. Then he turned his gaze to Jennifer, still lost in her dreams. He bent down, kissed her gently on the forehead, and quietly turned off the television. With Jack padding softly behind him, Robert made his way back to the kitchen, the events of the day—and the promise of tomorrow—swirling in his mind.

Chapter 30

"The Morning's Revelations"

It was a bright and early morning on the Chesapeake, the kind that promises a day full of hard work and salty breezes. Robert stood aboard his workboat, with Jack at his side, while Jennifer took her morning swim. The bay was calm, the water rippling gently as the sun stretched its golden fingers across the horizon.

As Robert kept an eye on his daughter, a familiar sight approached: Sydney McCullan's boat, gliding smoothly over the water. Sydney, as deft as ever, cut the engine and let his vessel coast alongside Robert's, the two boats aligning as naturally as old friends meeting at the dock.

Jack, ever hopeful, wagged his tail and licked his chops as Sydney reached into his pocket. A treat was sure to come.

"Good morning, Sydney. How goes all?" Robert called, his voice carrying easily over the quiet water.

Sydney, with a sly grin, tossed the treat to Jack, who snapped it up with the enthusiasm of a well-fed but never-satisfied dog.

"You've got a bit of a glow about you today, Robert," Sydney remarked, leaning back against his boat's railing. "Reckon you haven't heard the news?"

Robert, sensing something amiss, shook his head. "No, what's happened?"

Sydney's grin faded into a more serious expression. "Well, seems some folks took it upon themselves to make their feelings known last night—'bout that whole business with Chessie. I'm guessing they didn't bother you, but..."

Robert's brows knitted in concern. "Who? Watermen?"

"Likely," Sydney replied, his tone carrying a hint of resignation.

Robert pressed further. "What happened?"

Chapter 31

"A Night of Trouble"

The scene shifted in Robert's mind as Sydney recounted the events. Over at Scotty's place, the night had been anything but peaceful. Scotty, sitting at home watching television, had been blindsided by the explosion that tore through his floatplane, parked right outside. A fiery ball lit up the night, reflecting off the dark waters as the plane was reduced to charred remains.

"Blew it up," Sydney's voice echoed somberly in Robert's thoughts. "Same thing happened over at Larry's. His patrol boat went up in flames. Took them four hours to put that fire out."

Robert's eyes widened in disbelief. "Why didn't I hear about this?"

Sydney gave him a knowing look. "Word on the water is, you're on the other team now. Least, that's how most watermen see it."

"But we only did what the law allowed!" Robert protested, his frustration evident. "I can't represent a bunch of outlaws!"

Sydney nodded, understanding the tightrope Robert was walking. "Some folks don't see it that way, though. They had their own ideas of what should've been done with Chessie."

Robert turned to gaze out over the bay, his thoughts tangled like the nets in his hold. The weight of his decisions and their consequences bore down on him.

"You did right, son," Sydney said softly, breaking the silence. "You can't please 'em all, no matter how hard you try."

Robert sighed, still staring into the distance. Sydney's words were wise, but they did little to ease the turmoil within him.

"And," Sydney added, almost as an afterthought, "feel lucky they haven't come after you yet."

As Jennifer began her swim back to the boat, waving to Sydney from a good distance off, the older man gave Robert one final piece of advice. "If I were you, I'd keep a close eye on you and yours."

Robert nodded, the gravity of Sydney's words sinking in. As Sydney started his boat and began to pull away, he called back, "Stay well, young Williams!"

Robert watched as Sydney's boat motored slowly away, Jack barking after him. He reached down to calm the dog, his hand absently scratching behind Jack's ears as his mind continued to churn.

Chapter 32

"A Cold Reception"

Later that day, Robert found himself alone at The Crab Claw, trying to offload a couple of bushels of crabs. Craig came out to meet him, but without the usual handcart.

"Mr. Williams," Craig began, his tone more formal than usual, "Bill said we don't need any crabs today."

"Don't need any?" Robert echoed, a note of surprise in his voice.

"No, sir," Craig replied, his expression apologetic.

Robert frowned. "Well, I'll try the others then."

Craig hesitated, glancing back toward the shadows where Bill watched from a distance. "I doubt they'll need any either, Mr. Williams," he whispered, lowering his voice. "Look, just bring them by truck later. I'll buy them from you. Some of the others watermen refuse to sell to us if we buy from you—if you catch my drift?"

Robert understood all too well. The message was clear: he was being blackballed by his own community. He looked over at Bill, who quickly turned away, his posture stiff with disapproval.

"Thanks, Craig, but that won't be necessary," Robert said, his voice firm.

With a heavy heart, he opened the bushel and, one by one, dumped the crabs into the harbor.

Craig protested, "No, Mr. Williams, don't do that! You can't afford to lose so many catches."

But Robert was resolute. "We'll just let these little guys live a bit longer, "Craig. You know there's a shortage, don't you?"

As he finished with the first bushel, Robert picked up the second and did the same, letting the crabs scuttle back into the water. One particularly heavy crab made a bid for freedom, scurrying into a corner of the boat. Robert picked it up, examining it with a sad smile.

"Nice and heavy too," he muttered, almost to himself. "Heavy little fellow, aren't you?"

He gave the crab a gentle shake, as if expecting a response, then tossed it into the water with the rest. He turned back to Craig with a weary smile. "I'm done with this, Craig. Thank you for all your help. Hell, it was fun while it lasted."

Craig watched in silence as Robert started his boat, the engine's rumble filling the quiet dock. "I'm sorry, Mr. Williams," he called out, but Robert waved it off.

"It's Robert. You know that," he said, his voice carrying a hint of finality.

With that, Robert piloted his boat back toward his side of the harbor, leaving Craig standing on the dock, watching him drift away into the distance.

Chapter 33

"Preparing for the Evening"

As the afternoon turned into evening, the steam from Robert's recent hot shower filled his bedroom. Jack lay beside a neatly laid-out suit, watching as Robert shaved in front of the bathroom mirror.

The sound of the front door opening and Jennifer's voice calling out brought Jack's ears to attention.

"Dad?" Jennifer's voice echoed through the house.

"I'm in here," Robert replied, popping his head out of the bathroom just long enough to answer before disappearing back inside.

Jennifer opened the door, waving away the steam as she poked her head into the room. "What do you want for dinner?"

"I'm eating out tonight," Robert said, his voice muffled as he continued to shave.

Jennifer, puzzled, glanced at the suit on the bed. "Out? You?"

Robert's only response was a brief nod as he finished his grooming.

"With whom?" she pressed, her curiosity piqued.

"That biologist… what's her name," Robert answered, still not meeting her eyes.

"You know her name," Jennifer shot back, a mix of surprise and concern in her voice. "Bucky and I were going to go out tonight."

"That's fine, sweetie," Robert replied, finally emerging from the bathroom. "Grandpa Royals will be by to hang out."

Jennifer frowned. "Dad, I don't need a sitter too."

Robert looked at her, his expression softening. "I know. But with all that's been going on around here… I just need to know you're safe."

Jennifer didn't argue, but the worry in her eyes didn't fade as she watched her father prepare for an evening that seemed to mark the beginning of a new chapter in their lives.

Chapter 34

"An Evening of Change"

The evening had settled in, and the family room was dimly lit, with the television casting a soft glow across the room. Jennifer sat on the couch, her eyes fixed on the screen, though her mind was clearly elsewhere. The door creaked open, and in walked Robert, looking sharper than a new penny.

Jennifer's thoughts were a whirl of confusion and betrayal as she watched him enter, her inner voice echoing louder than the TV. That's when I knew nothing would be the same. My father was stepping out on my mother with that woman, and there wasn't a thing I could do to stop it.

Robert, oblivious to the storm brewing within his daughter, gave her a warm smile. "Remember, honey, I want you to lock the doors. Make sure you let Jack out to potty before you go to bed. I'll be home late, okay?"

Before Jennifer could respond, Sheriff Royals, or Grandpa Royals as Jennifer called him, entered through the back door, his presence as steady and reassuring as ever. Robert crossed the room to give him a hug.

"Hi, Hank. Thanks for coming by tonight."

Sheriff Royals waved off the thanks with a grin. "No problem, Robby. Where's my little girl?"

Jennifer, pouting but trying to mask it, gave a half-hearted wave to her grandfather. Robert, sensing her mood, bent down and kissed her on the head.

"Are you sure you're alright with this?" Robert asked, his voice tinged with concern.

Jennifer replied with a short, unconvincing, "Yep."

Robert frowned slightly but decided to accept her answer. "Jennifer's got a date tonight," he informed Sheriff Royals. "I want her back by 10, and bedtime's 11."

Sheriff Royals chuckled, playing along with the usual fatherly concerns. "Oh, I better go and get my guns, then."

Jennifer rolled her eyes at the playful threat.

Just then, a knock on the door set Jack to barking. Robert rushed to open it, revealing Linda, dressed nicely for the evening but not quite matching Robert's sharp attire.

Linda's eyes widened as she took in Robert's appearance. "Oh my, you look nice. I feel like I'm underdressed."

Robert shook his head, smiling. "Not at all, you look perfect. Come on in, I want you to meet my daughter."

Linda stepped into the house, her gaze sweeping over the tasteful decorations as she followed Robert to the family room.

"Linda, this is my daughter, Jennifer," Robert introduced.

Jennifer, still glued to the TV, barely acknowledged Linda's presence with a disinterested "Hey."

"And this," Robert continued, "is her grandfather, Sheriff Royals."

Sheriff Royals tipped his hat with a nod. "Pleasure, ma'am."

Jack, ever the friendly dog, jumped up to greet Linda, his tail wagging furiously.

"Jack, down!" Robert scolded, but Linda was quick to wave it off.

"No, that's okay! I love dogs!" she exclaimed, bending down to give Jack a rub on his belly.

Jennifer, still not bothering to look at Linda, quietly mimicked her words, "I love dogs," her lips moving in silent mockery.

Robert, oblivious to his daughter's disdain, smiled at the scene. "That's Jack. He loves to be loved."

Turning back to Jennifer, Robert added, "Remember, no little Buckies."

Linda, sensing the awkwardness, tried to be polite. "Nice meeting you, Jennifer."

"Right. Bye," Jennifer replied, still not tearing her eyes away from the television.

Seeing that the conversation was going nowhere, Robert gave Linda a slight nod, signaling it was time to leave. Linda smiled, though a bit uncomfortably, and followed him out. Jennifer watched them go, her expression unreadable.

As soon as they were gone, Jennifer grabbed the phone and dialed a familiar number.

"Hi, this is Jennifer. Is Bucky there?" she asked, her tone shifting to one of hopefulness.

Chapter 35

"A Change of Plans"

Meanwhile, in Bucky's room, the sounds of music filled the air as he lounged on his bed, flipping through a car magazine. His mother's voice called out from the other room, "Bucky, it's Jennifer."

Bucky picked up the phone, his voice cheerful. "Hi, Jenn."

"Can you come over sooner?" Jennifer asked, her voice betraying the anxiety she felt.

Bucky hesitated. "Well…"

"My dad is dating that biologist tonight. Can you believe it?" Jennifer added, hoping to spark some sympathy.

But Bucky's tone turned apologetic. "I can't go out with you tonight, Jennifer."

Jennifer's heart sank. "How come?"

"My father said I'm not even allowed to talk to you. He calls your father a traitor."

Jennifer's frustration boiled over. "So you're 18… it's up to you."

"I know. I'm sorry," Bucky replied before hanging up.

Jennifer stared at the phone, her disappointment palpable. "Great," she muttered to herself, feeling more alone than ever.

Chapter 36

"A New Beginning"

The late afternoon sun was dipping below the horizon as Robert drove Linda over the Chesapeake Bay Bridge. The fading light cast a golden hue over the water, creating a serene backdrop for their conversation.

Linda, always quick-witted, broke the silence. "I know why we're taking your car."

Robert glanced at her with a raised eyebrow. "Oh? Why's that?"

"So you get to take me home after dinner," she teased, flashing him a playful smile.

Robert chuckled, his mood lightening as they drove on.

As night fell, they arrived at a restaurant in Baltimore. Inside, a bottle of champagne was opened with a pop, and the waiter skillfully poured the bubbly into two glasses.

Robert and Linda exchanged toasts, their glasses clinking lightly in the intimate setting.

"To the safe capture of your monster," Robert joked, lifting his glass.

Linda laughed, raising hers as well. "To the future," she added with a wink.

The evening was a whirlwind of conversation and laughter. As they sat by the window overlooking Baltimore's Inner Harbor, the city lights twinkled in the distance, casting a magical glow over their evening.

"So," Robert asked, leaning in with genuine interest, "what's the next step with Chessie?"

Linda's eyes sparkled with excitement. "It's amazing how fast everything is happening. Just today, over 80,000 people came to see her. They've even set up a special glass-bottomed boat so people can watch her underwater."

Robert nodded, impressed. "I imagine she'll be a big attraction worldwide."

Linda smiled but then shifted the conversation. "Let's talk about something we can't see on the evening news."

"Oh? What would that be?" Robert inquired, curious.

"Let's talk about Robert Williams, or should I say Dr. Robert Williams?" Linda teased, her tone playful yet serious.

Robert feigned ignorance, looking around as if searching for the person she was referring to. "Who's that?"

Linda grinned, clearly enjoying herself. "I've done my homework. Harvard Law School graduate, Ph.D. in Philosophy, also at Harvard. Of course, my sources could be wrong, but how else could a waterman afford such a nice waterfront house, an $80,000 car, and a $1,500 Armani suit? Oh yes, let's not forget the $1,000 alligator shoes."

Robert took a sip of champagne, deflecting her probing questions. "That was a long time ago. Let's talk about the future."

"The future?" Linda mused, her smile widening. "The future is wide open. Especially now, with your help."

Robert's gaze softened as he looked into her eyes. "Let's toast to the future."

Linda hesitated, then clinked her glass against his, the sound echoing like a promise in the air. As the evening wore on, the music grew louder, and couples began to fill the dance floor.

Robert, feeling emboldened by the night, stood up and moved towards Linda, only to trip on the champagne stand and tumble forward. The bottle flipped through the air, spraying champagne over both of them.

Linda gasped, covering her face in shock, but Robert, sitting on the floor, burst into laughter. The waitstaff rushed to clean up the mess, but Linda couldn't help but join in the laughter, their shared clumsiness breaking the ice in the best possible way.

"Um, would you like to dance?" Robert asked, still chuckling.

"Are you asking me or the champagne stand?" Linda quipped, her laughter contagious.

As they rose to their feet, the waitstaff and nearby patrons chuckled along with them. Robert extended his hand to Linda with a mock formality. "Dr. Olson?"

Linda took his hand with a grin. "Dr. Williams."

Together, they made their way to the dance floor, where they danced a romantic waltz, lost in each other's eyes.

Chapter 37

"The Night's Quiet Moments"

Later, as they took a small harbor taxi across the calm waters, Linda shivered slightly in the cool night air. Robert, ever the gentleman, put his arm around her, pulling her close as the boat glided towards the glass-bottomed vessel where Chessie was temporarily housed.

As they approached, a security guard appeared, shining a bright flashlight in their faces. "Sorry folks, we open again tomorrow."

Linda shielded her eyes from the glare. "I'm Dr. Olson. I'm here to check on her."

The guard, realizing who she was, lowered the flashlight. "Oh, Dr. Olson. My apologies, ma'am. Didn't recognize you in the dark. It was quite a scare earlier with the bomb threat and all...."

The night was thick and close, with the kind of darkness that makes you feel like the world has folded in on itself. On the glass-bottomed boat, Linda stood with her arms crossed, her brow furrowed. "A bomb threat!" she exclaimed, disbelief and indignation coloring her voice. "Who in the world would want to hurt such a magnificent creature?"

The security guard, a man of few words and even fewer answers, shrugged his shoulders. "Beats me, ma'am. "Authorities were here for a few hours checking everything out."

Linda, ever the concerned scientist, pressed on. "How is she?"

The guard scratched his head, trying to find the right words. "Far as I can tell, Dr. Olson, she's just making the same noise over and over. Doesn't seem like no man-eater to me. Reminds me of back in '44, when our boat went down in the South Pacific..."

But before he could get into the thick of his tale, Linda and Robert were already descending the narrow stairs to the lower deck, leaving the guard to ramble on to himself. He noticed too late that his audience had moved on. "Well, if you didn't want to know, why'd you ask?" he mumbled to the empty air, shaking his head. "Women doctors... Lord!"

Chapter 38

"Below Deck"

Down below, the air was cooler, the space wide and open, made for tourists eager to peer through the large rectangular window into the murky harbor water. But tonight, the water seemed darker than usual, an inky void stretching out under the boat. The low, mournful moan of Chessie, echoing through the speakers above, filled the space with a haunting melody.

Robert paused, the sound pulling him in. "Is that her?" he asked, his voice soft.

Linda nodded, her fingers deftly adjusting the controls. "Mmm-hmm, listen closely."

Robert leaned in, letting the sound wash over him. He touched the speaker, as if trying to feel the sadness that poured out of it, then turned to the window, where the creature hovered in the blue glow of the underwater lights. The sight took his breath away.

Linda, noticing his awe, stepped closer. "We can monitor her vital signs from here, and even play it back for the visitors," she explained, her voice a mix of pride and concern.

Robert shook his head in amazement. "I can't believe this was all set up so quickly."

Linda smiled, though it didn't quite reach her eyes. "Without this display, we wouldn't get the funding we need to continue our research."

She led him to a wall at the back of the room, covered with sketches and plans. "The money she brings in will help build a proper home for her, a place where she'll be safe, and where we can study her in a controlled environment."

Robert's eyes scanned the elaborate drawings, plans for a grand addition to the National Aquarium. "It's a shame she has to be caged."

Linda's face softened. "I know. But we can't afford to lose her. Think of how long she's existed without man ever discovering her."

They both turned back to the window, gazing at the creature that seemed both ancient and otherworldly.

"When I look into her eyes," Linda whispered, "I can tell she's far more intelligent than we are."

Robert nodded, the sadness in Chessie's moans tugging at his heart. "Her cries sound so sad."

Linda sighed. "I think she's still grieving the loss of her child."

The room fell silent, save for the low hum of the boat and Chessie's plaintive calls.

Chapter 39

"A Change in the Tide"

After a long pause, Linda broke the silence. "May I ask you a personal question?"

Robert glanced around, a hint of humor in his eyes. "Depends on where that guard is."

Linda smiled, though her tone was serious. "If I overstep, you'll tell me, right?"

"Sure," Robert replied, curious now.

"Why is a Harvard Law School graduate posing as a waterman in Saint Michaels?"

Robert's face grew thoughtful. "I was raised in Saint Michaels. Met my late wife there. My job took us to Manhattan, where I made a seven-figure income as a corporate lawyer. We had everything we ever dreamed of."

As Robert spoke, his mind drifted back to a rainy night in Manhattan, fourteen years ago. The streets glistened under the city lights, but there was danger lurking in the shadows.

Shelley, his wife, was driving home in her new Mercedes when she was ambushed by two young hijackers. They shouted at her, banged on her car, and tried to drag her out. In her panic, Shelley reached for a can of pepper spray and managed to fend off one of them. But the situation escalated, and in a moment of blind rage, one of the hijackers pulled out a gun and fired, ending her life in an instant.

Back to the Present.

Robert's voice trembled as he recounted the story. "My wife resisted. She wasn't street-smart enough to know better, and she was shot and killed."

Linda's eyes filled with sympathy. "I'm so sorry."

"They didn't even take the car," Robert continued, his voice heavy with regret. "It's taken me a long time to come to terms with it. The hardest part is knowing that if I hadn't been so successful, she might still be alive. She would still be Jennifer's mother."

Linda shook her head. "That wasn't your fault. You were just doing what any man would do for his family—providing the best life you could."

Robert sighed. "That's how it seems, but I think I did it more for the money than for my family. Now, I have a great life here with my daughter. In Manhattan, I rarely saw her. One day she was born, and the next, she was two years old and motherless."

Linda's heart ached for him. "You've dated since then, haven't you?"

Robert shook his head. "No. That's probably why Jennifer wasn't very welcoming tonight."

Linda nodded, understanding now. "I don't blame her. The poor girl. She must hate my guts."

"Jennifer doesn't hate anyone," Robert reassured her. Then, trying to lighten the mood, he asked, "So, what's your story?"

Linda smiled wistfully. "Been married and divorced. I love my work so much, I haven't found a man who understands."

Robert moved closer, his voice gentle. "Any men in your life now?"

Linda burst out laughing, the tension of the moment dissolving. "George. I left him back at the restaurant, playing with his..."

She laughed harder, wiping tears from her eyes.

Robert grinned. "George, huh?"

"Yes," Linda gasped, still laughing. "He was playing with his silly little computer, buying stocks and things on eBay. I bet he doesn't even know I'm gone."

Robert chuckled, sharing in her amusement. "Where did you go?"

Linda's laughter faded as she looked out at Chessie. "To save her."
A Moment of Connection

Robert followed her gaze, but his eyes were on Linda, not Chessie. "She is beautiful," he said, though it was clear he wasn't talking about the creature.

Linda, oblivious to his meaning, nodded. "Wouldn't you just want to give her a big hug and a kiss?"

Robert's voice was soft. "Very much so."

Without another word, Robert turned Linda toward him and kissed her deeply, a kiss that seemed to melt the world away. It was a moment of pure magic, at least until the security guard cleared his throat.

"Ahem, ahem," the guard interrupted, standing awkwardly in the doorway.

Robert and Linda parted reluctantly, their eyes still locked on each other.

"Sorry to interrupt your research," the guard mumbled, "but we've got a boat heading back if you want to catch it."

With one last glance at Chessie, Robert and Linda walked toward the exit, their hearts lighter despite the weight of their memories. As they passed the guard, he rolled his eyes, muttering something about young folks today.

The guard turned off the interior lights, leaving only the soft blue glow that illuminated Chessie's lonely figure. Her moans continued, echoing through the empty waters as Robert and Linda sailed back to shore.

Chapter 40

"Overlooked"

Beneath the surface, Chessie's moans echoed into the darkness, a song of sorrow that seemed to reach into the very depths of the bay. But then, another sound emerged, a different moan, deeper and more resonant.

Chessie spun around in her confined space, her eyes widening as she glimpsed a larger form moving through the murky water—a male of her kind, drawn by her calls.

The male circled the net, his powerful body cutting through the water with ease. Chessie followed his movements, her eyes filled with hope. He took hold of the chain in his strong jaws and pulled with all his might, trying to free her. But the net held firm, its iron grip unyielding.

For a moment, the two creatures floated eye to eye, their silent communication filled with the sadness of separation. The male let out a low, mournful sound before turning away, disappearing into the murk from which he came.

Chessie watched him go, her heart heavy with loss. She floated there, motionless, her moans fading into the silence of the deep.

Chapter 41

"On the Front Porch"

The night air was thick with the kind of stillness that settles on small towns after the day's troubles have finally worn themselves out. Jennifer sat on the front porch, Sheriff Royals beside her, both absently petting Jack, the family dog. The silence between them was broken only by the distant hum of crickets and the soft rustling of leaves. But that peace shattered when Robert's voice floated up the path, mingled with the light laughter of Linda.

Jennifer's eyes, red and swollen from crying, darted up as they drew nearer. She quickly tried to compose herself, brushing at her cheeks.

Robert, noticing her distress, spoke first. "What are you still doing up at this hour?"

The Sheriff, sensing a moment best left between father and daughter, patted Jennifer's shoulder and quietly retreated into the house.

Jennifer didn't answer, her gaze dropping back to Jack, her tears welling up again.

Linda stood to the side, silent, her own heart heavy with concern.

Robert, his voice now filled with worry, knelt beside his daughter. "Honey, what's wrong?"

Linda, realizing this was a moment that might need privacy,

gestured that she should leave, but Robert shook his head slightly, asking her to stay.

Jennifer struggled to speak, her voice choked with sobs. "I... I did what we always do. I let Jack out to go potty... and..."

Robert leaned closer, gently urging, "And what, sweetie?"

Jennifer's tears spilled over as she continued, "He didn't come back like he usually does, so I went outside to look for him."

Robert's concern deepened. "Did someone hurt you?"

She shook her head, her voice breaking. "No. I found him lying in the grass... shaking."

Robert's eyes widened as he looked down at Jack.

Jennifer continued, her words barely a whisper. "Grandpa called Dr. Gardner, but by the time he got here, it was too late."

Robert looked up at Linda, his face etched with pain. Linda, tears in her own eyes, knelt beside Jack, gently examining him.

"He died... here... on my lap," Jennifer sobbed, unable to hold back any longer.

Her father pulled her into a tight embrace, his own tears now falling freely.

Jennifer added, her voice trembling, "Dr. Gardner thinks he was poisoned. He took some blood. I... I couldn't find you." He took some blood. I... I couldn't find you."

Robert hugged her tighter, his voice thick with sorrow. "I'm so sorry, sweetie. I'm so, so sorry."

Linda, standing nearby, reached out to Robert, her hand finding his in a quiet show of support.

Chapter 42

"In the Kitchen"

Later, in the dimly lit kitchen, Sheriff Royals and Robert stood by the counter, talking in hushed tones. Linda sat at the table, a cup of coffee cradled in her hands, her thoughts heavy. Jennifer remained on the porch, still petting Jack, now silent and still.

"This town's changing, Robby," the Sheriff said, his voice low but firm. "First the patrol boat, then the plane, and now this? And Bucky telling Jennifer he isn't allowed to see her anymore? Things are getting out of hand."

Robert's eyes flashed with anger. "What did you say?"

The Sheriff waved it off for now. "Not the time, Robby. You need to keep your family close, keep everything you care about in sight. Don't give them another chance to strike."

Robert glanced out the window at his daughter, his heart aching at the sight of her grief. "It breaks my heart that this could happen here, in our little town."

The Sheriff nodded, his face grim. "We'll find who did this. I promise you that."

Robert walked him to the door. "Please, Hank, keep us informed."

The Sheriff gave a nod. "I'll be by first thing in the morning, Robby."

Chapter 43

"By Jack's Grave"

As the night wore on, Robert and Jennifer laid Jack's body to rest in a small grave dug in the backyard. The moonlight cast long shadows over the solemn scene as Jennifer knelt by the grave, tears streaming down her face. She leaned in, giving Jack one last kiss on his now lifeless head, placing one of his favorite treats beside his nose.

Linda, wanting to comfort Jennifer, stepped forward to offer a hug, but Jennifer recoiled, her voice sharp with pain. "Don't touch me! This is all your fault. Just leave me alone!"

The words cut through the night like a knife. Jennifer turned and ran back into the house, leaving Linda standing there, frozen in shock and guilt.

Robert started to call after Jennifer but stopped himself, knowing his daughter needed time. He turned to Linda, pulling her into his arms as she trembled with the weight of her emotions.

"She's just very upset right now," Robert whispered, trying to soothe her.

Linda shook her head, her voice barely audible. "She's right, in a way. If I hadn't interfered..."

Robert watched as Jennifer disappeared into the house, his heart torn between his love for his daughter and the growing bond with

Linda.

Linda took a deep breath, pulling away slightly. "I guess I'll call you tomorrow."

Robert nodded, still staring at Jack's grave. "I'm sorry about all this, Linda. I really did have a great time with you tonight."

Linda managed a faint smile, though it didn't reach her eyes. "I did too. Good night, Robert."

"Good night," he replied, his voice soft as he watched her walk to her car, his heart heavy with the evening's events.

As Linda drove away, Robert wandered down to the dock, his footsteps slow and heavy. He stood at the edge, staring out at the moonlit river, the water sparkling in the night, reflecting the turmoil in his heart.

Chapter 44

"The Morning After"

The next morning, Sheriff Royals stood in the kitchen with Robert, both nursing cups of coffee. The weight of the previous night's events hung between them like a dark cloud.

"Any idea who could have done this?" Robert asked, his voice edged with frustration.

The Sheriff shook his head. "Could be anyone at this point. Half the town seems to be against us now. But you did the right thing, Robby. Sometimes people just don't think."

Robert sighed, rubbing his temples. "The Bannister family lost the most. I can't imagine what they're going through."

The Sheriff nodded, his expression somber. "Daniel's still lying in bed, sedated to the point where he can't even say hello, let alone orchestrate this mess. It's likely some of his friends."

Robert leaned against the counter, the weight of everything pressing down on him. "I've been meaning to visit Daniel, see how he's doing."

The Sheriff placed his coffee mug down, readying himself to leave. "That might be a good gesture, Robby. But remember, keep your family close. We'll step up patrols around your house until we sort this out. You call me directly if anything else happens."

Robert nodded, leading the Sheriff to the back door. "Thanks, Hank. I appreciate it."

Chapter 45

"In the Backyard"

As they stepped outside, the Sheriff paused, taking in the view of the quiet backyard. "It's nice having you back here in Saint Michaels, Robby. You've done a lot for this town, and I'd hate to lose you because of all this."

Robert offered a small, grateful smile. "Thanks, Hank."

The Sheriff hesitated, then asked, "So, what's the story with that biologist?"

"Linda?" Robert replied, caught off guard.

"Yeah, Linda." The Sheriff shifted uncomfortably, looking out at the water. "I know I've never said this before, but I've been meaning to for a long time now."

Robert turned to face him, sensing something important was coming.

The Sheriff took a deep breath. "Shelley's mother and I... we never blamed you for what happened, you know? She was so happy with you. You did more for her than anyone else could have."

Robert's eyes filled with tears as he listened, his heart breaking all over again.

The Sheriff's voice wavered, but he kept going. "I know we haven't talked much over the years, but... well, you know how it is. We both suffered a tremendous loss. God, I miss my little girl."

Robert couldn't hold back his emotions any longer. "I'm so sorry, Dad."

The Sheriff pulled him into a tight hug. "You didn't do it, son. It could've been you. And Shelley would be back here missing you. But the difference is, I would have been there for her, kicking her in the ass to get on with her life—something I didn't think I could say to you, Robby. I felt like it wasn't my place."

The Sheriff pulled back slightly, forcing Robert to meet his gaze. "Son, I want you to get on with your life. Shelley would want you to as well. We all know you loved her very much. But your life isn't over. Get on with it before it is."

Robert nodded, hugging the Sheriff one more time, both men fighting back tears.

Their tender moment was interrupted by a shout from the dock.

"Hello!" Sydney McCullan called out, waving as he approached.

The Sheriff and Robert broke apart, quickly wiping their eyes.

"You okay, son?" the Sheriff asked, his voice steady again.

Robert nodded, taking a deep breath. "Yeah, Dad. I'm okay."
The Sheriff gave him a firm nod. "Then get busy living. I've got work up to my ass."

The Sheriff and Robert exchanged a look that spoke volumes—one of those rare moments where words would have only gotten in the way. Sheriff Royals gave a nod, a silent message of understanding, before turning on his heel and heading toward the front of the house.

Robert watched him go for a moment, then turned to see Sydney McCullan waving him over. Without hesitation, Robert made his way toward his old friend, eager to see what was on his mind.

"Top of the mornin' to ya, Syd," Robert called out, his voice carrying that familiar warmth.

Sydney, ever the old sea dog, gave a half-smile. "Hope I wasn't interrupting anything important."

Robert shook his head, his smile fading just a touch. "Just tying up some loose ends."

Sydney's eyes narrowed slightly, sensing something was amiss. "You weren't down at the docks this morning. I missed you. Where's Jack?"

At the mention of Jack, a shadow crossed Robert's face. Sydney, always prepared, reached into his pocket and pulled out a treat meant for the dog. But Robert's answer stopped him cold.

"Jack was poisoned last night, Syd," Robert said quietly, his voice heavy with grief. "Hank's trying to find out who did it."

Sydney's hand froze mid-air, the treat suddenly feeling like a lead weight. "Is he... is he alright?"

Robert's eyes dropped to the ground. "Jennifer and I buried him last night."

A look of sorrow flashed across Sydney's weathered face, and he tossed the treat into the water with a sharp flick, his anger rippling out with it. "Those bastards. I've had it up to here with them. All of them."

Robert placed a calming hand on Sydney's shoulder. "It's not all of them, Syd."

But Sydney wasn't so sure. His mind was made up, his voice laced with bitterness. "What did your dog ever do to them? This town's gone mad."

Robert sighed deeply, the weariness of the last few days etched into his features. "I'm giving it up, Syd. It's clear they don't want me representing them any longer."

Sydney looked at him, eyes wide with disbelief. "Most of the guys are on your side, Robby. The ones responsible, they'll be fished out."

Robert glanced over at his old workboat, the memories tied to it suddenly feeling more like an anchor than a lifeline. "Can you follow me to the Maritime Museum, Syd? I think it's time to retire this old girl, and I may need a lift back."

Sydney looked at Robert, then at the boat they'd both known so well. "You're really giving in?"

"No, just moving on," Robert replied, a sad smile tugging at the corners of his mouth. "I won't be needing her anymore."

Sydney, ever the optimist, clapped Robert on the back. "Well, how about we stop over at The Carpenter Street Saloon after? A man can't make a big decision like this on an empty stomach."

Robert chuckled, despite everything. "It's only ten in the morning, Syd."

Sydney grinned, his eyes twinkling. "Not in Ireland, laddie!"

Chapter 46

"At the Maritime Museum"

The morning sun shone down on the Saint Michaels Maritime Museum, casting long shadows across the boats docked nearby. Robert stood, shaking hands with the Museum's Director, as Sydney looked on, his expression a mix of disbelief and quiet understanding.

"Just a few short days," Jennifer's voice echoed in her mind as she walked home through the familiar streets of Saint Michaels. "In just a few short days, my father caught a dinosaur, let go of Mom, and gave his boat away to a museum. Our lives were turned upside down."

Chapter 47

"Back at the House"

Jennifer trudged up the steps to the front porch, feeling the weight of the world on her young shoulders. She tried the door, but it was locked. With a sigh, she dropped her book bag and fumbled for the key. Once inside, the silence greeted her—a stark contrast to the whirlwind of thoughts swirling in her head.

"Dad?" she called out, half-expecting to see him napping on the sofa like he always did. But the house was empty, the only sound the steady ticking of the old grandfather clock.

She wandered into the kitchen, glancing out the sliding glass door. The boat was gone. Panic started to bubble up when she heard a familiar voice.

"Hi, sweetie."

Jennifer jumped, spinning around to see her grandfather standing in the doorway. Relief flooded her, but it quickly gave way to tears.

"You scared me, Grandpa."

The Sheriff walked over, wrapping his arms around her. "Are you okay?"

Jennifer's tears spilled over, her voice a shaky whisper. She wasn't okay. she didn't know who she was anymore. She didn't know what to do.

The Sheriff's heart ached for his granddaughter, seeing how much she was struggling. "Your dad went to the hospital to check on Daniel. Things will all work out, you'll see."

But as much as she wanted to believe him, Jennifer wasn't so sure. The world she knew was slipping away, and she felt powerless to stop it.

Chapter 48

"Daniel"

The steady beeping of the heart monitor echoed softly in the small, sterile room, a monotonous reminder of the fragile thread upon which life dangled. Daniel lay in the hospital bed, his face pallid, and his breath labored, aided by the thin tubes that snaked into his nostrils, delivering the oxygen that kept him tethered to this world. His eyes, once bright with mischief, now flickered weakly under the burden of pain and medication.

Robert entered the room, his steps cautious as if afraid to disturb the delicate balance of life and death that seemed to hover in the air. The nurse, a no-nonsense woman in a crisp uniform, ushered him in with a soft whisper.

"You just missed his mother," she said, her voice low, respectful of the solemn atmosphere. "He's only just started regaining consciousness today. We've been keeping him heavily medicated for the pain."

"Can he speak yet?" Robert asked, his eyes fixed on the frail figure of his friend.

"Yes," she nodded, "but it takes a lot out of him. Please keep the visit short; he needs his rest." With that, she slipped out of the room, leaving the two men alone.

Robert approached the bed, forcing a smile to his lips, a gesture meant to be reassuring, though he wasn't entirely sure who needed the reassurance more—himself or Daniel.

Despite his weakened state, Daniel managed to summon a grin, the same roguish smile that had charmed many and infuriated just as many others. "They had to build me a new pecker," Daniel croaked, his voice raspy and weak but laced with that familiar humor. "Want to see it?"

Robert was caught off guard by the quip, unsure whether to laugh or cringe. But as Daniel chuckled—a sound that quickly dissolved into a rough cough—Robert couldn't help but join in, his laughter tinged with relief that his friend's spirit had not been entirely dimmed by his ordeal.

"We're all lucky you made it through this, Danny," Robert said, his voice steady, though his heart clenched with the gravity of the situation.

Daniel's smile softened, the bravado fading as he nodded. "Yup. The doctors say I'll be up on my stubs in no time." His eyes, however, told a different story—one of fear, uncertainty, and the haunting realization of all he had lost.

He glanced around the sterile room, his smile wavering as reality settled in. "Shit, how in the hell am I going to pay for all of this crap?"

"Don't worry about that," Robert replied, his voice firm, squeezing Daniel's hand as if to transfer some of his strength into his friend's weary body.

Daniel's eyes filled with a mix of gratitude and sorrow as he met Robert's gaze. "I told you that damn Chessie was out there," he said, his voice thick with emotion.

"You told the whole world, Danny," Robert replied, his tone soft, understanding the weight of those words.

A tear escaped Daniel's eye as he continued, his voice trembling. "We didn't want to kill the thing, Rob. We tried to let it go. Cost me my legs. And my son." His voice broke, and he looked away, the pain too much to bear.

Robert squeezed Daniel's hand harder, offering what little comfort he could.

Daniel's expression hardened with a newfound resolve. "I might have died too," he muttered, his eyes steely with determination. "Makes me want to get out of here and start living again."

Robert felt a surge of admiration for his friend. Even in the face of unimaginable loss, Daniel was ready to fight for whatever life he had left. But before he could respond, the nurse reappeared, her presence a reminder of the limits of this visit.

"Time's up, Mr. Williams. He needs his rest," she said, moving to the other side of the bed, her hands busy with the routine tasks of caregiving.

Robert nodded, reluctantly about to release Daniel's hand. "You let me know if you need anything, okay? Anything, Danny."

Daniel nodded, his grip tightening briefly in silent gratitude before he let go. Robert took a step back, preparing to leave, when a sudden, loud smack echoed through the room.

Robert turned, startled, to see the nurse rubbing her backside, her expression one of shock mixed with mild exasperation.

"Oh! Mr. Bannister!" she exclaimed, stepping out of the reach of Daniel's mischievous hand.

Daniel, his face a mix of boyish glee and cough-induced regret, chuckled softly, his laughter turning into a fit of hacking coughs. As he composed himself, he offered Robert a salute, a gesture that was both playful and poignant.

Robert, shaking his head with a smile, returned the salute before exiting the room, his heart a little lighter for having seen a glimmer of the old Daniel, still fighting, still living, even in the face of such overwhelm.

Chapter 49

"Linda's Call"

Jennifer lay sprawled on the couch, dressed in nothing but one of her father's old Harvard T-shirts, the fabric oversized on her small frame. The television flickered with the light of some mindless program, more background noise than entertainment. The shrill ring of the phone cut through the room's otherwise idle hum. Jennifer sighed, sat up, and reached for the receiver.

"Hello?" she answered, her voice flat, as if even this small task was a burden.

On the other end, Linda's voice chirped with a brightness that only irritated Jennifer further. "Hi, Jennifer? This is Linda. How are you doing?"

"Fine," Jennifer replied, the single syllable hanging in the air with a chill.

"Is your father home? I really need to speak with him," Linda continued, her tone hopeful.

"No," Jennifer said simply, and without another word, she slammed the receiver back onto the cradle.

Linda blinked in confusion, staring at her phone as if it had betrayed her. "Jennifer? Hello?" But the line was dead. Sighing, Linda pressed redial.

Once more, the phone rang in Robert's family room. Jennifer picked it up, her voice clipped as she answered, "Hello?"

"Hi, Jennifer," Linda's voice came through again, though now with a note of apology. "I think my connection was bad. Sorry about that. I really need to speak—"

But before she could finish, Jennifer cut the call again, leaving Linda to stare at her phone in disbelief. "She hung up on me," Linda muttered to herself, closing her phone with a sigh.

Jennifer tossed the receiver aside and slumped back on the couch just as her father entered the room, the energy he carried with him too buoyant for her current mood.

"Are you ready to go out?" Robert asked, noticing her sprawled on the couch.

Jennifer didn't bother to hide her skepticism. "Where's the boat, Dad?"

"I donated it to the museum today," Robert replied, matter-of-factly. "You're not going out like this, are you?"

She stared at him, trying to gauge his seriousness. "You were serious?" she asked, her disbelief evident.

"Yes!" Robert confirmed with a chuckle. "Get something on. We're going to C-Street."

Her expression brightened, the sulkiness vanishing in an instant. "Carpenter Street Saloon?" she asked, excitement creeping into her voice.

"Yes, now go get dressed," Robert said, laughing as Jennifer planted a quick kiss on his cheek before sprinting out of the room to change.

Chapter 50

"C-Street"

The Carpenter Street Saloon was a staple of Saint Michaels, a two-story building that stood proudly along the town's main thoroughfare. It was the kind of place where locals gathered to share stories, gripe about the weather, and enjoy a hearty meal with a drink—or several.

Inside, Robert and Jennifer found themselves standing near the bar, waiting for a table to clear. The familiar hum of conversation and clinking glasses filled the air. Robert glanced down at his daughter, a question on his mind.

"Any calls for me today while I was out?" he asked, his tone casual, though his eyes searched hers for any hint of deception.

Jennifer hesitated, weighing her options before answering with a simple, "No."

Roger, the bartender, spotted them from the other end of the bar and made his way over, a warm smile on his face. "Hi, Mr. Williams. Jennifer, haven't seen you for a while. Want something to drink while you're waiting?"

Before Robert could respond, Jennifer beat him to it, her tone teasing. "A couple of beers, Roger!"

Robert shot her a look of mild disapproval, but Jennifer just grinned, while Roger chuckled at the exchange.

"Give the young lady a soda and me a Jack straight-up," Robert said, turning back to Roger.

"The heavy stuff," Jennifer muttered under her breath, but Robert pretended not to hear, his attention already elsewhere.

As Roger moved to prepare their drinks, Sydney McCullan entered the bar, his eyes scanning the room until they landed on Robert. He seemed genuinely surprised to see him there, his voice rising above the din of the crowd.

"Either I've had too much to drink or not enough," Sydney called out as he made his way over, a grin on his face.

Robert just smiled, his eyes twinkling with amusement.

Sydney clapped him on the shoulder and turned to the bartender. "Roger, give me two double Scotch on the Rocks! Make sure to cover the ice..."

"Yes sir, Mr. McCullan!" Roger replied with a grin, already setting to work.

"Thanks, Syd, but we already ordered," Robert said, though he appreciated the gesture.

"Those aren't for you, laddie," Sydney replied with a wink. "They're both for me!"

Laughter bubbled up around them as Roger delivered the drinks, and Sydney raised his glass high. "Here's to a long life and a merry one. A quick death and an easy one. A pretty girl and an honest one. A cold drink—and another one!"

They all clicked their glasses together, smiles all around, as they took a sip of their drinks. Sydney, of course, downed his first one in a single gulp, much to Jennifer's wide-eyed amazement.

"My gosh, Sydney," she exclaimed.

"A bird can't fly with one wing, lassie," Sydney quipped as he quickly finished his second drink, causing Robert to shake his head in amusement.

The saloon was in full swing now, mixed with tourists and familiar faces and lively chatter filling the space. Sheriff Royals, making his rounds, passed through and greeted Robert and Jennifer with a warm smile.

"Good to see you two out and about," the sheriff said, tipping his hat to Jennifer. "Where's your friend, Rob?"

"She's working, I imagine," Robert replied, a touch of nonchalance in his voice.

The sheriff gave him a knowing smile and then turned to Jennifer. "Are you okay?"

Jennifer nodded, grateful for the concern. "Yes. Thank you, Grandpa."

"Don't drink too much," the sheriff added with a chuckle, ruffling her hair before moving on.

Just as things seemed to settle, Sydney, still waiting for his next round, suddenly caught sight of something on the bar's television. His voice cut through the room, loud and clear. "Isn't that your girlfriend, Robby?"

Robert turned toward the television, his face flushing as he saw Linda's image on the screen. Jennifer, less amused, rolled her eyes.

Roger, the bartender, couldn't help but jump on the moment. "Mr. Williams has a girlfriend?

And just like that, the bar erupted into a playful chant, the patrons all joining in unison, "Wooh!"

Robert's face turned crimson, his embarrassment clear, while Jennifer covered her ears, not wanting to hear any more. Roger, sensing their discomfort, quickly called for the crowd to quiet down.

"All right, all right, quiet down so we can hear!" Roger shouted, turning up the volume on the television.

The crowd gradually settled, their attention now on the screen. Jennifer kept her hands over her ears, while the rest of the room focused on the news broadcast. Chessie's image filled the screen, and the voice of the news anchor came through, serious and somber.

"The Chessie saga takes yet another turn today as Dr. Linda Olson prepares to address the press," the anchor announced. "We believe she will make a plea to release Chessie back into the bay. As you may already know, Chessie has been responsible for the deaths of five people and the maiming of one in an incident that took place in Saint Michaels Harbor…"

The crowd, loyal to their town, cheered at the mention of Saint Michaels, their pride evident even in the face of such grim news.

The footage shifted to scenes of angry protesters, their signs reading "Stuff Willy!" and "Let her Die!" The divide in public opinion was clear, and the tension in the room grew thick as the anchor continued.

"Many here are not in favor of turning the dinosaur back into their local waters."

The room fell silent, everyone waiting to see what would happen next, the fate of Chessie hanging in the balance.

The scene at Baltimore's Inner Harbor was charged with anticipation.

Linda approached the temporary podium set up for her, the weight of the moment heavy on her shoulders. The crowd before her was a sea of faces—some curious, others skeptical, many hostile. She took a deep breath and began to speak, her voice steady despite the tension crackling in the air.

"Ladies and gentlemen," she started, her tone measured and calm, "I am here today to inform you that the Plesiosaur, the creature we've all come to know as Chessie, is slowly dying; she simply will not eat in captivity. In my professional opinion, if we are to save Chessie, and perhaps learn more about her life outside of captivity, we must set her free."

The crowd responded with a mix of cheers and boos, a cacophony of opinions clashing in the open air. A newspaper reporter, standing near the front, couldn't hold back his question.

"If we let her go, what do you think is going to stop her from killing again?" he shouted, his voice slicing through the noise.

Linda held her ground, meeting the reporter's gaze. "We do not believe that Chessie will kill unless provoked. We believe the harm she caused was out of instinct; she was acting as any mother would—to protect her baby."

Just then, a hooded elderly woman began pushing her way through the throng, her movements slow but determined. The crowd shifted, allowing her passage as she approached the podium. Pulling back the hood of her black cloak, the woman's face came into view—lined with age and sorrow, yet resolute with purpose.

Another reporter, undeterred by the woman's interruption, pressed Linda, "But didn't you say that you were going to release her back into the Bay?"

Before Linda could respond, the elderly woman spoke up, her voice quivering with emotion. "Do you know who I am, lady?" she demanded, her eyes fixed on Linda.

Linda hesitated, trying to place the woman, but her face held no recognition.

The woman's voice rose, cracking with pain. "That damn thing killed my grandson. If you let it go, it'll kill again."

Linda opened her mouth to assure her, "I assure you—" but she never finished the sentence. In one swift, terrible motion, Mrs. Bannister drew a pistol from beneath her cloak and fired, the sound of gunshots tearing through the air. Linda staggered as the bullets struck her chest, the force of the impact dropping her to the ground.

Back at the Carpenter Street Saloon, the lively chatter and warmth evaporated in an instant. The room froze, eyes wide in horror as the scene unfolded on the television.

Robert's face drained of color, his earlier enthusiasm giving way to shock. Jennifer, who had been covering her ears moments before, now opened her eyes, drawn by the sudden stillness in the room.

Every gaze in the bar turned to Robert, who stood as if rooted to the spot, his mind struggling to process what he had just witnessed.

On the television screen, Mrs. Bannister was tackled by three Baltimore City policemen, her face twisted in a grimace of rage and grief. The crowd around Linda erupted into chaos, people running and screaming, while others rushed to her side, desperate to help.

The news anchor's voice trembled with the weight of the moment. "It appears that Dr. Olson has just been shot. The police have taken the woman into custody. We don't yet know if anyone else was injured, but we can only hope Dr. Olson…"

Robert's hands shook as he fumbled for his wallet, his movements mechanical, almost detached. The people around him parted instinctively, allowing him space as he placed a twenty-dollar bill on the bar. Roger, the bartender, motioned for him not to pay, but Robert ignored the gesture, his mind already elsewhere.

Sydney reached out and patted him on the shoulder, his own expression grim. Without a word, Robert turned and left the bar, Jennifer following closely behind. The rest of the patrons began to murmur amongst themselves, the disbelief palpable. Sheriff Royals shook his head, as though trying to dispel a nightmare.

Meanwhile, at the Baltimore Inner Harbor, paramedics worked frantically to keep Linda alive. Her eyes were closed, her body limp as they placed an oxygen mask over her face and carefully lifted her onto a stretcher. The sound of sirens pierced the evening air as they rushed her to the waiting ambulance.

Chapter 51

"Visitation"

As dusk fell over the Chesapeake Bay, Robert drove with a single-minded focus, his car speeding over the Preston Memorial Bridge. The sun had long since dipped below the horizon, leaving the sky a deep, bruised shade of purple. Jennifer sat silently beside him, her eyes fixed on her father's profile. She noticed a tear slip down his cheek, and without thinking, she reached for his hand.

She never saw her father cry for anyone but my mother before, she thought, her heart aching for him. When Robert glanced over at her, he managed a sad smile, though his eyes were heavy with grief.

Hours passed in the sterile waiting room of Johns Hopkins Hospital. Robert sat rigidly in a plastic chair, his eyes never leaving the door that led to the emergency rooms. Jennifer watched him, wishing she could do something—anything—to ease his pain.

The minutes crawled by, turning into hours. Jennifer brought her father a cup of coffee, but he barely acknowledged it. He hadn't moved from his seat, his gaze still locked on that door, as though willing it to open and bring good news.

Much later, the waiting room was eerily quiet. Jennifer had finally drifted off to sleep on a nearby couch, her small form curled up under a thin hospital blanket. Robert, however, remained in his chair, his posture unchanged, as the weight of the world seemed to press down on him.

The early morning sun cast a gentle glow over the hospital, its light filtering through the tall windows, promising a new day. Inside, the atmosphere was one of quiet anticipation. Robert, with a huge stuffed toy replica of Chessie cradled in his arms, walked down the long, sterile hallway. Jennifer followed behind him, her footsteps nearly silent, her mood as subdued as the muted colors of the hospital walls.

The nurse, a kind-faced woman with a no-nonsense air, met them at the door to Linda's room. "She's not out of the woods yet," she warned softly. "Keep it brief."

Robert nodded, the concern etched on his face deepening as he glanced at Jennifer. She leaned against the wall, her posture stiff, her expression distant. It was clear she had no desire to visit Linda, but there they were, and there was no turning back.

Inside Linda's room, the atmosphere was unexpectedly bright. The moment Robert stepped in, Linda's face lit up with a warm smile that seemed to chase away the sterile chill of the hospital. Her eyes sparkled as she saw the stuffed dinosaur in his arms, a smile playing on her lips despite the strain of her injuries.

"You look much better than you did last night," Robert said gently, trying to mask his own lingering fear. "You had us worried."

Linda's smile widened, and she motioned for him to look around the room. Robert's eyes followed her gesture, landing on an impressive array of flowers that filled the space with color and fragrance, turning the room into a temporary garden.

Feigning mock indignation, Robert asked, "Who sent you all these?"

Linda simply pointed at him, her smile teasing.

Robert's brow furrowed in playful confusion, and he pointed at himself in question.

Linda nodded, her fingers gently brushing a tear from his cheek, a tender touch that spoke volumes.

Robert leaned in, placing a soft kiss on her forehead, then another on her nose, his affection clear in every gesture. The moment was tender, sweet, and full of unspoken words. But just as Robert's lips left her skin, the door opened with a quiet creak, and the nurse stepped back in, a knowing smirk on her face.

"I knew better than to leave you two alone in here," she chided with a grin. "Visit's over, sugar lips."

Linda and Robert exchanged a rueful smile, knowing their time was up.

"There'll be plenty more time for that, Romeo," the nurse added, waving him toward the door.

Reluctantly, Robert obeyed, stepping out into the hallway, but not before stealing one last glance at Linda.

Chapter 52

"You're Not My Mother"

As Robert spoke quietly with the nurse about Linda's condition, Jennifer saw her chance. With both of them distracted, she slipped into Linda's room, her presence unnoticed until she stood beside the bed.

Linda, admiring the stuffed Chessie, was startled when she looked up to see Jennifer standing there, her face shadowed with something unreadable.

At first, Linda offered a smile, but it faltered when she saw the stern expression on Jennifer's face.

Jennifer moved closer, her gaze flicking to the heart monitor, then back to Linda. The room seemed to grow colder as she drew nearer, her face just inches from Linda's.

"I hate you," Jennifer whispered, her voice cold and cutting.

The words hit Linda like a blow. She could only stare, her heart rate quickening, the monitor beside her betraying her rising panic.

"Since you came into our life, everything is totally different," Jennifer continued, her voice wavering as her stern expression began to crumble.

Her eyes filled with tears, but she pressed on. "You know, I never really got the chance to know my mother that long, I was less than ten when she died, but I do know she loved my father very much. And my father still loves her."

A tear rolled down Jennifer's cheek, mirrored by one from Linda. The tension between them thickened, heavy with unspoken pain.

"I love my father very much too," Jennifer choked out, "and now my father loves you."

She wiped her tear away roughly, resisting Linda's gentle attempt to help. But when Linda reached out, her touch was so tender, so full of understanding, that Jennifer's resolve cracked.

"You can never be my mother," Jennifer said, her voice breaking.

Linda nodded, her own eyes filled with tears, understanding the truth of those words. She tried to speak, but the effort was too great. All she could do was shake her head in agreement, her heart breaking for this young girl.

Just then, Robert appeared in the doorway, his expression softening as he saw the scene unfolding. He started to step forward, but Linda raised a hand, silently asking him to stay back. He obeyed, his heart aching as he watched his daughter struggle with her emotions.

"I also wanted to say I'm so sorry," Jennifer sobbed, her voice barely above a whisper. "If I didn't hang up on you..."

Linda mustered all her strength to lift a trembling finger to Jennifer's lips, gently silencing her. "No," she whispered, her voice hoarse but firm. "It's not your fault."

For a moment, Jennifer fought the wave of emotions that threatened to overwhelm her. But then, unable to hold back any longer, she broke down, collapsing into Linda's arms. Her sobs were raw, filled with all the grief and confusion she had been holding inside.

"Please don't die," Jennifer cried into Linda's shoulder. "It would hurt my father so much."

A tear slid down Linda's cheek as she held Jennifer close, her hand stroking the girl's hair in a gesture of comfort. Robert, standing in the doorway, wiped at his own eyes, his heart full of love for the two most important people in his life.

Chapter 53

"The Aquaholic"

Time passed, as it always does, and the years slipped by.

Once again, Jennifer, now a young woman, was dozing at her desk, her head resting on her folded arms. The room was small, the afternoon sunlight casting long shadows across the floor. A gentle hand on her shoulder shook her awake.

"What are you doing?" a familiar voice asked.

Jennifer blinked, rubbing her eyes. "Resting my head," she replied, her voice still thick with sleep.

Linda, standing over her, shook her head with a smile. "I see."

Just then, Robert walked into the room, a smile on his face. "Hey, you two," he called, "I think we're coming up on them again."

Jennifer jumped up, excitement replacing the drowsiness as she followed Robert out the door. Linda lingered for a moment, watching Jennifer's retreating figure with a smile of her own. Then, with a quick kiss from Robert, she joined them, ready for whatever adventure lay ahead.

The "Aquaholic", a grand 40-foot research yacht, cut through the gentle swells of the open sea, its sleek body gliding effortlessly across the waves. Jennifer, her heart racing with excitement, dashed to the back of the vessel, where Daniel lounged in his wheelchair, sunbathing beneath the warm rays of the sun. With a determined grip, she began wheeling him toward the bow of the ship, navigating carefully along the narrow starboard side.

In her thoughts, Jennifer's voice echoed softly, a reminder of the journey that had brought them all to this moment. After many complications, Linda finally left the hospital in time for her to see Chessie's release into the open ocean. The memories of those difficult days still lingered, but today was about celebration.

Daniel, ever the vigilant observer, had his binoculars trained on the horizon, scanning the waters. Robert helped make this possible by cutting a deal with Daniel Bannister to plea in Chessie's defense in return for paying his medical bills. It was a deal born of necessity, but one that had brought them all closer.

As Jennifer guided Daniel past a ladder, she glanced up to see her father,

Robert, and Linda making their way up to the flying bridge of the yacht.

A sudden, playful smack echoed across the deck, drawing Daniel's attention. He grinned as he saw Linda clutching her bottom, giving Robert a mock scolding look before hurrying up the ladder with a little more speed. Robert, unable to suppress his amusement, met Daniel's gaze with a knowing smile, while Jennifer, turning bright red, tried to hide her embarrassment.

"Oh!" Linda exclaimed with mock indignation.

"Dad!" Jennifer admonished, half embarrassed, half amused.

A memory from a year ago surfaced in Jennifer's mind, as vivid as if it had happened only yesterday...

The day was bright and filled with joy. Linda, resplendent in a beautiful white wedding dress, and Robert, looking every bit the proud groom in his tuxedo, stepped out of the quaint gray church in Saint Michaels. The whole town had turned out for the wedding, and as they emerged, a shower of rice fell upon the newlyweds. The happiness was infectious, and Jennifer, beaming in her bridesmaid gown, felt a surge of pride.

She remembered, how proud she was to be her bridesmaid...

As the happy couple climbed into a horse-drawn carriage, their faces glowing with love, Jennifer's heart swelled with joy. Her grandfather, Sheriff Royals, and her grandmother stood beside her, their smiles as wide as hers, watching Linda and Robert begin their journey together.

The present moment brought her back as the family leaned over the flying bridge, eagerly searching the waters below.

"Where are they, Sydney?" Linda called, her voice tinged with excitement.

Sydney McCullan, the seasoned captain of the Aquaholic, steered the craft with practiced ease. "Just off our starboard bow," he replied, his eyes scanning the sea.

Robert was about to join them on the deck when a small bark caught his attention. He paused, looking around for the source of the noise.

"Who made that noise?" he wondered aloud.

At the base of the ladder, a little Black Lab puppy, Junior Jack, the family's newest companion, was doing its best to climb up after Robert, its tiny tail wagging furiously. The puppy whined and whimpered, desperate to be with its new favorite person.

Chuckling, Robert climbed back down to scoop up the eager pup.

"Come on, Junior Jack," he said, lifting the squirming ball of fur into his arms and carrying him up the ladder. When Robert reached the top, he found Linda already focused on the sea. Chessie, the male, and their new baby were gliding gracefully alongside the yacht, navigating the waters of the Gulf Stream with an elegance that left everyone in awe.

Linda secured a grant to study the Plesiosaur family with a boat Robert bought,

Jennifer finally reached the bow with Daniel, who was smiling as he watched the dinosaurs porpoising beside the boat, their movements a perfect harmony with the ocean's rhythm.

Daniel is a guest on the vessel as long as he stops asking people if they want to look at his artificial penis. Robert threatened to feed the rest of him to Chessie if he ever tried to show it to anyone.

Looking up at her father and Linda, Jennifer saw the happiness radiating from them. They were as content as anyone could hope to be. Sydney, noticing Jennifer's thoughtful smile, gave her a salute. Jennifer returned the gesture, her heart swelling with a mixture of love and gratitude.

She turned her gaze back to the dinosaurs, watching as they moved effortlessly through the water. Chessie and her family squealed happily as they swam, the baby weaving excitedly around its parents, full of youthful energy.

Since Chessie has come into their lives, everything seems to flow effortlessly and naturally...like the water and the winds, feeling a deep connection to the gentle giants below.

The baby dinosaur circled its parents, a symbol of the life and love that had been rekindled in all of them. Without her showing up, they may never would have learned what true love is. How delicate and extinct it has become...as fragile as life itself.

Jennifer lifted her face to the sky, the wind playing with her hair. Joyful tears filled her eyes as she thought of her mother, certain that somewhere, she was smiling down on them.

Linda rested her arm on Jennifer's shoulder, "Are you okay?"

Jennifer smiled and leaned into Linda's embrass and
whispered "I know my mother is smiling, wherever she is...I do remember her smile."

Linda's smile agreed.

As the Aquaholic sailed onward, the family and their ancient companions continued their journey together, a journey that had brought them all closer, bound by love, life, and the mysterious beauty of the never ending world around them.

The End